More Wise Men of Helm

More Wise Men of Helm and their Merry Tales

SOLOMON SIMON

Edited by HANNAH GRAD GOODMAN

Illustrated by STEPHEN KRAFT

BEHRMAN HOUSE, INC.

To my grandchildren

DEENA, NATALIE, SUSAN *and*

DANNY, BILLY & DAVID

The people of Shedlitz and Warsaw will tell you, "How does it happen that the city of Helm is full of fools? Because it is written in The Holy Scriptures: 'God watches over the simple.' Now, if the simpletons were scattered all over the world, even He would find it difficult to keep an eye on them, for no one can foresee what a simpleton will do. So, He in His wisdom gathered all the fools in one city, where it is easy for Him to watch over them."

The Helmites retort, "Whoever says that the people outside of Helm have sense proves he is a fool. It is expressly stated in the Talmud: 'The world was delivered into the hands of the fools.' "

Well, I could never decide who is right, Helm or the rest of the world. Let the reader decide.

Contents

The sages of Helm

HELM HAS GREAT PHILOSOPHERS AND SCIENTISTS as well as Talmudic scholars. The most outstanding of them is Pinya the Deep-Thinker, who can demonstrate by pure logic that Warsaw is Helm and Helm is Warsaw. Then there is Shloime the Scientist, also known as Shloime the Mathematician. He can prove to you, for example, that a triangle may have four angles. And Berel the Beadle, who is a Helmite only on his mother's side, but now and then has ideas as brilliant as a true Helmite's. Of note also are the rising logician, Reuben the Water-Carrier; and Abba, Mayor Gimpel's grandson, who is a sort of a Helmite prodigy.

These three sages have a great following. They discuss many important questions with their disciples. In the long winter nights they can usually be found at the nook behind the brick stove in the synagogue. The group is called "the sages of the *lizanke*"—"*lizanke*" being the edge of the stove, where the elderly people like to sit and doze in the winter.

During the cold of winter, Berel the Beadle lights a fire in the brick stove. When the stove is hot enough, he puts potatoes in it to bake. The sages sit in the corner, each with a fine, mealy, baked potato in his hand, and exchange gems of wisdom.

Novices who wish to attain the exalted status of the noted sages must pass a test. They are asked three questions—questions that may seem simple, but which very

few outside of Helm have ever answered correctly. They require a special kind of wisdom—the wisdom of Helm.

The first may be a question of chemistry. For example, "Let's suppose you want to sweeten a glass of tea. Therefore, you put sugar in it. Then you take a teaspoon, and mix and mix. You stir till nothing is seen of the sugar. Now, the question is, what sweetens the tea, the sugar or the teaspoon?"

3

The novice is given plenty of time to think over such a question. If he is a person of deep understanding and great wisdom he will reply, "It is the teaspoon." He will be asked to explain, of course.

"The fact is, we don't need the sugar to sweeten the tea. We put the sugar in so we'll know when to stop stirring. When the sugar is melted, we know that the stirring has sweetened the tea and it's time to stop."

You can imagine the applause which greets such an answer!

The second question is likely to be in the realm of mathematics. "How much are four and three, and another four and three?"

A person of true Helmite spirit and logic will reach the correct answer: "Eleven."

"How do you arrive at this figure?" he will be asked.

If he is wise enough to remember a certain example, he will be able to reply, "I call to your attention the case of Keila, a widow with four children, who married the

widower Motta, with four children. Later she bore him three children. Therefore, Keila had four children by her first husband and three children by her second husband. Motta also had four children from his first marriage and three from his second."

At this point, everybody in the room is following the brilliant reasoning with bated breath.

"Still, there are only eleven children. This proves that four and three, and four and three are eleven."

This triumph of reason wins the would-be sage a try at another question—the final and most difficult of all. It might be something like this: "Why are the summer days warm and the winter days cold?"

Complicated as this problem is, no sage of Helmite calibre would fail to arrive at the correct conclusion. "During the winter the stoves are lit and give off heat. This heat gradually warms up the air so that by the time summer comes, the days are hot. In the summer, the stoves are used very little—only for cooking. Therefore, the air cools gradually, month by month. When winter arrives, it is actually freezing, so the stoves are lit and the whole process is repeated all over again."

This shows how completely logical and rational the Helmites are.

After a novice has had his hour, the sages settle down to explore new and uncharted frontiers of knowledge. In a typical dialogue the philosopher, Pinya, once pointed

out: "You know, sages of Helm, that God in His grace created a beautiful and orderly world. As it is written in the Holy Scriptures, 'To every thing there is a season, and a time to every purpose under the heaven: a time to plant and a time to pluck up that which is planted; a time to keep silence, and a time to speak; a time to weep, and a time to laugh.'

"God in His mercy also compensates a handicapped person for his defects. If a man is blind, his sense of hearing is sharper and his sense of feeling is keener. If a man is deaf, his sense of sight is more clear."

"Pardon me, Pinya," Shloime the Scientist retorted, "how do you know? You're not blind or deaf. What's your proof of this?"

Unruffled, Pinya answered calmly, "You can learn by observation. Take, for instance, a man who is blind in one eye. Everybody knows that he can see better than a man with sight in both eyes."

"You make irresponsible statements," Shloime the Scientist answered angrily. "What do you mean, everybody knows that a man blind in one eye can see better than a man with two good eyes! I don't know it!"

Pinya chuckled. "You're just spiteful, Reb Shloime. It's simple. The man with one eye can see the other man's two eyes, while the man with two eyes can see only one eye of the half-blind man."

Everybody stared, wide-mouthed. "There is another

proof. If a man has one short leg, his other leg is always longer. It compensates for the shortness of the first leg."

Shloime nodded his head. "You know, each to his own field! I'm good with figures, but you, Reb Pinya, are clever in pure philosophy. Your logic is overwhelming!"

Reuben the Water-Carrier, the most promising of the disciples, said to the great scholars timidly, "I'm young and inexperienced. I'm not a philosopher like Reb Pinya, nor a scientist like Reb Shloime. Therefore, I've always been afraid to express my opinion. But, Reb Shloime, a great idea struck me. May I tell it to the forum?"

"Go ahead, Reuben. The night is young and the potatoes are warm and tasty."

"You, Reb Shloime, once pointed out how unfair our society is. The rich can buy whatever they want for cash, and besides that, on credit. They can even borrow as much money as their hearts desire. All they have to do is sign a note! But the poor are doubly handicapped. They haven't any money and no one honors their promissory notes. Shouldn't it be just the opposite? The promissory notes of the rich shouldn't be honored, because they have money and don't need credit. But the poor, who haven't any money, should be given credit out of necessity.

"All Helm agreed with you. Then along came Berel the Beadle, who argued that the poor can't be trusted, because when it's time to pay the promissory note, they won't have the money. 'The sums they borrowed will be

lost, and the rich who lent them the money will also become poor,' Berel said. 'The reform you suggest will merely increase the number of poor people. Who will gain by it?'

"Well, Berel's argument is sensible, but I can refute it easily," Reuben declared.

"Fiddlesticks!" interrupted Berel the Beadle. "My argument is ironclad. And look who wants to refute it—a water-carrier!"

"I don't mean to contradict the esteemed Berel," Reuben said hesitantly, "but I think his objection can be overcome. I propose a law which will restrict the rich to buy only for cash. Credit shouldn't be given them, and their promissory notes shouldn't be honored, for they don't need either. However, the poor should be able to buy everything they want on credit, and their promissory notes must be honored, because they need both. But we know that when the time comes to pay for the goods bought on credit, or to return the borrowed money, the poor won't be able to pay. Granted! What will happen then? The rich will also become poor. But is that a calamity? Not at all! When the rich become poor, they won't need money either, because then their credit will be good!"

Shloime and Pinya smacked their lips with delight, as if they had tasted a good piece of *gefilte* fish. "A plain water-carrier of Helm has more sense in his little finger

than a non-Helmite philosopher has in his head! Now all we have to do is convince the rich that their wealth is not a necessity for happiness!"

8 When the two sages had finished their praises of Reuben the Water-Carrier, Zelig the Wagoner arose. Zelig not only is poor, but also childless, which in Helm is considered much worse than being a cripple. "Sages of Helm," he said, "with your compassion for the poor and the downtrodden, you give me courage to ask you something which has puzzled me many years. Just look at me! I'm forty years old, but my face is as smooth as a freshly-scrubbed baker's kneading board. There's not a single hair on my face! By heredity I should have a luxurious beard. You all remember what a fine, thick, long beard my father had. How is it that I, his son, am beardless? What became of the law of heredity?"

Pinya smiled wisely. "Zelig, you are beardless *because* of heredity. But you don't take after your father. You resemble your mother, and . . ."

Zelig did not let him finish the sentence. "You're right, Reb Pinya!" he cried. "I do resemble my mother! As a matter of fact, I have her brown eyes. It *is* a matter of heredity! She, also, had no beard!"

The question once arose: Is it more important to know how to write or how to read? It was finally resolved that it is much more important to know how to write. The logic is clear. If you write a letter, it doesn't matter if

you don't know how to read it, because you can always find a man who knows how to read. What Jew does not know how to read the prayer book?

The sages also treated the difficult question: Which is more important, the sun or the moon? After much controversy the opinion of Pinya the Philosopher was accepted: namely, that the moon is the more important. This is because the sun shines by day, when it is light; but the moon shines at night, when it is dark. It is then an absolute necessity!

You must admire the Helmites for one thing: They have an intellectual curiosity. They don't take anything for granted. They want to know, as the Jewish proverb has it, where the legs grow from. One winter night they considered where the rain comes from.

When Pinya the Philosopher posed the question, Berel the Beadle retorted angrily, "Pinya, that's a stupid and impious question! It's a question a heretic would ask! What do you mean, where does the rain come from? God gives rain, as the Scriptures say: 'And did they not say in their heart, let us now fear the Lord our God that gives us the early rain and the late rain in the proper season.' Do you deny it?"

"Who denies the truth of a verse in the Holy Bible?" Pinya answered disparagingly. "Of course, the Lord God makes the rain fall! But my question is, what is the process?—how does God do it? Quiet, don't jump up! God

makes everything grow and bloom. Still, we do know that a tree grows from a seed. Different seeds bring forth different kinds of plants. So I want to know where the rain comes from."

"Well, it's described in many books," Shloime explained. "The clouds are like sponges. They descend into the ocean, and when they touch the water they absorb it, as a sponge does. When they have absorbed all they can, they ascend to the sky. Then a wind comes along and drives them against each other. They bump so hard that the water is squeezed out of them and begins to fall as rain."

"How do you know that it is so?" Berel the Beadle piped up.

"Don't you see the rain falling?" Shloime answered, calmly. "What other proof do you want?"

Shloime the Mathematician

AMONG THE PROMINENT CITIZENS OF HELM, the most celebrated is Shloime the Mathematician. He rose to fame after Pinya returned from his journey to Warsaw because of a mix-up with a pair of shoes. It was Shloime who had brought the fire engines to Helm, as well as the barrels full of Warsaw water to put out fires. He did all this without mishap. But he became really famous after he was already a greybeard. His renown came late in life because he was a taciturn man who seldom talked.

Once he was asked, "Reb Shloime, don't you get tired of being silent?"

"Yes," he answered. "I do get tired of keeping silent, so I rest up by not talking."

He was always absorbed in scientific theories and mathematical problems. Since he had no solutions to the problems, he did not talk about them, except to himself, silently. "What kind of an order is that in the world? Why does God send snow and frost upon the world in the winter time, which is a hard time for people as it is?

Couldn't He send the frost and the snow in summer time, when it's hot? I say it's unjust!"

Shloime was far from good-looking. He was once asked, "How is it that a fine brain like yours is lodged in such an ugly body?"

"I was born a beautiful boy," was his answer, "but the midwife mixed me up with another child. So I am not myself. I am the good-looking one. The other boy, who is not me, is the ugly one."

Shloime was mostly interested in mathematics, for numbers are the only unchangeable things. Three times three are always nine, and two times two are always four. This is the one stable thing in the world, and a man might well model himself after it, by being stable and unchangeable, too. He should be firm and unyielding, and keep his word under all circumstances.

But eventually, Shloime began to have doubts even about numbers—which is why he became famous.

One fine summer day he was alone in his store, deep in thought. He had a small shop filled with odds and ends of hardware and tools, plus old furniture and utensils which he would buy at auctions.

It was late afternoon when Shloime stood in the store, much perturbed. Figures are not as stable as people think! He wrote on a slate, "Three times three are nine." Good! But what if you remove the multiplication sign? "Then it can, if I want it to, become six; and if I want to . . ."

At that moment, a nobleman appeared and spied an old lamp with a tall stem. It was made of copper, green with age, and the base was fashioned of fine black marble.

"How much for the lamp, Shloime?"

Shloime, busy with the slate, muttered, "Two threes can be six if you put an addition sign between them . . ."

"All right, I like the lamp. I'll give you six ducats."

13

Shloime did not hear the nobleman. He went on with his calculations. "But if you put the two threes side by side, like this—it's thirty-three!"

The nobleman was a bit peeved. "That's quite a jump, Shloime, from six to thirty-three ducats, but my wife likes antiques. Let it be thirty-three ducats!"

Shloime was not even aware of the nobleman's presence. "But on the other hand," he continued, "if you write one, one and one, then another one, one and one, it's really only six ones. But if there isn't a sign between them, like this, 111111, it becomes one hundred and eleven thousand, one hundred and eleven! Worse yet, and even more illogical, if you put three ones, one after another, like this, 111, it comes to one hundred and eleven. It's three, and also one hundred and eleven!" He flung the slate to the floor. "One hundred and eleven is the last figure I bother with!"

"Wait a minute, Shloime!" exclaimed the nobleman. "You're going too far! First you said six ducats, then thirty-three, and now you want one hundred and eleven. It's ridiculous!"

Then Shloime became aware of the nobleman and heard him say, "It's ridiculous!"

"You agree with me?"

"Of course, I agree with you! Who ever heard of raising the price of an old lamp from six ducats to one hundred and eleven?"

Shloime looked at him, bewildered. "What lamp?"

"This!" The nobleman pointed to the lamp in the corner. "Thirty-three ducats is more than enough."

Shloime shrugged his shoulders. "This lamp is priced one ducat and it's not worth any more."

"But I offered you thirty-three just a minute ago, as you asked. Then you changed your mind and raised it again to . . ."

Shloime interrupted him. "Sir, my figures had nothing to do with the lamp. The lamp's not worth more than one ducat. I was working on a mathematical problem."

The nobleman paid the ducat, took the lamp and said, "Well, if I live to be a hundred, I won't fathom the wisdom of Helm! But I like you, Shloime. I wish there were more like you. You keep your word and always tell the truth. Always, I say!"

Since then Shloime has been famous as a man who keeps his word. Once he says something, he does not change his mind. But the real demonstration of his strength of character came a year later, in the matter of the open door.

Go, close the door!

WHEN IT IS WINDY IN HELM IT IS WINDY, FOR the city is open on three sides. The gale blows so hard and fierce, it often tears the coat clean off a man. All the roofs of Helm are bound with wire to protect them from the storms. The doors are sturdy and fastened on heavy metal hinges.

One wintry night, Shloime the Scientist and his wife went to sleep. Suddenly the door was blown open by a gust of wind. It kept banging open and closed, with a deafening clatter.

"Didn't you lock the door?" Shloime asked his wife.

"No," she answered.

"Go and close the door."

"Why should I? You close it!"

Shloime replied, "Because I said, 'Go and close the door.' And when I say something I keep my word."

"I'm your wife. If you're a man who keeps his word, I must be worthy of you, and I have to keep my word, too. I said, 'You go and close the door,' so you have to do it."

"Well," answered Shloime, "I like your stubbornness. You're a fit wife for an honest man like me. Therefore, the situation is complicated. I can't shut the door because I gave my word not to, and I can't tarnish my reputation. I can't make you lock it because you're my wife. As the saying goes, when the husband is a Rabbi, the wife is a Rebbetzin: so, if I can't lock the door because of my word, you can't break your word either. Let's agree that whoever speaks first must close the door."

"Agreed!"

The rain turned to snow, the wind into a hurricane. The door kept swinging and banging, and the house became cold. The husband and wife shivered under the feather quilts and could not sleep. Still, neither of them closed the door.

Before dawn the storm quieted a bit, and two thieves went out to see what they could pick up. When they passed Shloime's house and saw the open door, they entered. Shloime and his wife heard voices.

"Look, we didn't have to break in! The door's open and the house is full of copper utensils and silver and clothes. Come on, let's pack! We're in luck tonight."

"Not so loud! Maybe they're sleeping somewhere. You'll wake them up."

"Don't be stupid," answered the first thief. "The door makes a racket to wake the dead. There's nobody home. Come on, let's get busy."

Husband and wife clearly heard the thieves begin to clean out the house. They worked at a leisurely pace. The wife heard the clang of the copper pots and pans as they went into the thieves' bags. When one thief admired her beautiful teakettle, she began to weep silently, but she didn't stir. Shloime heard the thieves empty the bookcase. He bit his lips in vexation, but did not move.

After the thieves had finished packing, one of them paused. "You know, I'm hungry. Let's light a fire and have a bite."

"Are you crazy? Somebody might hear us."

"Who? what? when?" laughed the first. "If anybody was here, the racket we made would have waked him long ago. They must have gone away for the night."

So the thieves stayed and prepared a meal. They had a fine repast, and whatever they could not eat, they took along with them. Nothing remained in the house but the furniture.

"It's too bad we didn't know beforehand about this," the first thief remarked regretfully. "We could have brought a horse and wagon and carted everything away."

The thieves left with both hands loaded, so they did not close the door.

Morning came. Shloime and his wife rose and dressed. They looked around and saw four bare walls and the furniture. Everything which could be packed in bags had been carried off. Neither of them uttered a word.

The wife saw that there was not a crust of bread, that the teakettle was gone, and not a pot was left to cook cereal for breakfast. She looked at Shloime and thought, "Poor thing, he must be hungry! I'll go to a neighbor and borrow something for breakfast. It's a wife's duty to feed her husband."

She ran out and, of course, did not close the door.

She stayed a while at the neighbor's. Shloime sat on a bench, sulking. Things hadn't turned out right. His wife had not closed the door, and thieves had cleaned out the house. There was not a book left to meditate on. Why, they had even stolen the prayer book and the *talith,* so that he could not go to the synagogue!

In those days barbers did not have shops, but went from house to house to look for work. A passing barber noticed the open door and wandered in. He looked around and saw Shloime sitting on the bench, deep in thought.

"You know, Reb Shloime," the barber said, "you need a haircut badly. Shall I cut your hair?"

Shloime did not answer. Well, according to the Talmud, silence means consent. So the barber spread his tools on a table, removed Shloime's hat, and began to cut his hair. He trimmed and sang merrily, and after a while, asked, "Well, Reb Shloime, how do you like it? I think I did a good job!"

Shloime was boiling with anger. "Who asked him for a haircut?" But, of course, he didn't answer, for he would have had to close the door. He grunted but did not speak.

"Well, I see you want a closer trim! It's all right with me, I can do it."

The barber snipped and chattered, snipped and chattered. Shloime became angrier and angrier, but not a word escaped his lips.

So the barber cut and cut, and trimmed and trimmed, until Shloime resembled a shorn sheep. "Do you like the haircut now?"

Well, what could Shloime do? He couldn't say that he didn't need a haircut, didn't want a haircut, and looked ridiculous with his head shorn so close.

The barber again misinterpreted his silence. "I know what you want, Reb Shloime! You want your head shaved, so that the hair will grow better later on. You have quite a bald spot."

When there was no answer, the barber soaped Shloime's head and shaved it clean. His pate shone like a full moon!

When the barber had shaved his head, Shloime was still quiet. The barber looked at him, and squinted one eye. "You know, Reb Shloime, with a clean shaven head like this, your beard looks wild and bushy. Your sidelocks are also a bit too long for a shaved head. I'll trim the beard and the sidelocks."

Shloime wanted to jump up and scream, "What kind

of a pest are you? Who asked for a haircut? Who asked
you for a trim or a shave? Now, you want to touch my
beard! How will I show myself among my people with a
trimmed beard? Am I one of the heretical Jews of Warsaw? I am a Helmite, and a Helmite does not trim his
beard under any circumstances!"

But, of course, he did not say it. If he had uttered one word he would have had to close the door.

So the barber trimmed Shloime's beard and sidelocks. He always stopped and asked whether it was enough, but Shloime did not answer. He remained silent. In short, all the barber left of the beard was a little goatee, less than the size of a shaving brush.

Then he turned to Shloime. "Now, Reb Shloime, you owe me ten kopeks, and I must say you got your money's worth. Pay me."

No, I cannot describe Shloime's hot anger; the paper would burn up. But what could he do? He couldn't argue the price, or he would have to close the door. So he glowered in silence.

The barber began to plead. "Reb Shloime, I'm a poor man and I worked hard. Pay me what's coming to me! Look how clean I shaved your head and how neatly I trimmed your beard! You look ten years younger."

Shloime's face became red with rage, but he did not utter a word.

The barber became angry. He gathered his tools, and erupted, "Wait, I'll teach you a lesson, you stubborn, silent donkey!"

He went to the chimney, took some soot and blackened Shloime's head and face. Then he stormed out of the house and did not close the door.

When Shloime's wife returned, she found her husband

sitting on the bench, his head shaven, his fine beard gone, and his pate and face black with soot. She forgot the agreement. Dropping the uncooked breakfast and the borrowed utensils on the floor, she wrung her hands, and cried out, "Oh, God, what did they do to you, Shloime?"

Our scientist rose calmly from the bench and spoke in a quiet voice. "Now, woman, you spoke first. Go and close the door!"

23

A dead man who talks

THE TOWN OF HELM STANDS IN A WOODED region, which begins on the western slope of the mountain and stretches for hundreds of miles. Timber from these woods is transported to the faraway cities of Danzig and Koenigsburg. The Helmites are good lumberjacks and loggers, for they learned the trade young.

Last winter was a good season for logging. The weather was cold, dry and windless—perfect for felling trees. The snow was heavy on the ground, making it a good sleigh road and easy to haul the timber to the river.

One morning Avrom, the son of Berel the Beadle, was taken to the woods for the first time, to learn lumberjacking. The foreman, a Litvak, advised, "The first thing a lumberjack must learn is the proper handling of the ax. So, for a start, trim the branches of the trees."

The foreman meant, of course, the branches of the felled trees. But Avrom climbed a tree, sat on a long, sturdy bough and began to chop at it.

When the foreman noticed what Avrom was doing, he

came running and shouting, "You Helmite fool, you're sitting on the branch you're cutting! When the branch breaks, you'll fall and break your neck! Come down, you fool! You'll fall and get killed."

"But you told me to trim the branches of the trees."

"The *felled* trees, not the *standing* trees! Get down, get down!"

Avrom scratched his head and thought, "He's surely a confused man, that Litvak foreman. First he tells me to cut down the branches and then . . . he might change his mind again. First, I'll finish what I started." And he continued chopping with his ax.

The foreman became frantic, but before he could do anything the branch broke and Avrom fell into the deep snow.

The foreman and four others came running. Avrom lay motionless, hands and feet stretched out, eyes closed, his lower lip bleeding.

The Litvak foreman looked at him. "I'm afraid the fool killed himself. Come on, put him in a wagon! We'll take him into Helm to a doctor. Maybe he only lost his consciousness."

The men put Avrom in a wagon, and the foreman and another Litvak drove toward Helm.

Both Litvaks were strangers in Helm. Therefore, when they came to a fork in the road they didn't know which way to turn. "Let's ask the miller which road goes to Helm," the foreman suggested. "The mill isn't far from here."

Immediately, Avrom sat up in the wagon and said, "Why do you have to ask the miller? I know the way. Turn to the right."

As he finished his say, he promptly dropped back, and lay motionless.

The foreman jumped from the wagon, joyfully. "Thank God, you're alive, Avrom!"

But Avrom lay motionless and did not answer. The foreman shook him. "Avrom, did you faint again?"

"No," replied Avrom. "I didn't faint. I'm dead."

The foreman stood, open-mouthed. "What do you mean, you're dead?" he stammered.

Avrom lay stretched out in the wagon and didn't move a muscle. The foreman shook his head. "He fainted again."

Avrom sat up again, indignantly. "No, I didn't faint! I'm dead. You said I'd fall down and break my neck and die. Well, I did fall off the tree, so I'm dead."

"But you're talking!"

Avrom stretched out again.

The second Litvak turned to the foreman. "This is your first winter here, so you don't know the Helmites. He can't be contradicted by a stranger. Let's get him to Moishe the Miller. Moishe has lived in Helm for years and he'll know what to do."

They brought Avrom to Moishe Litvak. The miller heard the story calmly. "If he says he's dead, he's dead. Lay him out on the floor as we do with the dead, and . . ."

"But he's alive!" protested the foreman. "I heard him talk just before!"

"I heard the story," answered Moishe, impatiently. "You can't expect him to believe you. Avrom is perfectly

logical. Lay him on the floor, cover him with a black cloth, and put lighted candles around him. Then send for Shloime the Scientist. Whatever Shloime says, Avrom will believe."

Shloime walked into the house and looked at Avrom laid out. "Is he dead?"

"He says so," answered the miller, matter-of-factly.

"Well," said Shloime, "if Avrom says so, it's true. I know him. He's an honest man. He never told a lie."

"But if he's still talking," protested the foreman, "he must be alive. How can a dead person talk?"

Shloime eyed the foreman, mockingly. "So he talks! That's no proof he isn't dead. Our tradition tells us that dead people do talk. It is written: 'The lips of the scholars in the grave murmur when their names are cited.' We need more definite proof that Avrom isn't dead or we'll have to bury him."

"You mean to tell me that you'll bury him if there isn't any other proof that he's alive?" cried the foreman in horror.

Shloime became impatient. "I can't understand you, Litvak. You told him that if he fell down, he'd get killed. He did fall down, so he's dead. Are you now going back on your word?"

Avrom sat up and waved the black cloth aside. "Reb Shloime, that's what I told him! I must be dead. After all, I *did* fall down."

Shloime waved him aside. "Don't mix in! You're not involved in this. I'll talk to you later."

The foreman sat down and mopped his brow. Shloime took a chair, sat down and bent over Avrom. "Avrom, do you have any pain?"

29

"No," answered Avrom, "I'm dead. How can I have pain?"

"You're right," answered Shloime, "but I want to make more tests before you are buried. Usually a feather is put in a dead man's nostrils. If he is really dead he can't breathe, so the feather does not move. Then a mirror is put to his mouth, if he is really dead there is no breath, and there is no moisture on the glassy surface. So lie still and let me verify your death by these crucial tests."

Avrom answered, "Well, whatever you decide, Reb Shloime, I'll abide by. Everybody knows your integrity. You're an honest man."

So Avrom lay still and held his breath while Shloime conducted the tests. Well, the feather did not move and the mirror did not get foggy. Shloime said, "Yes, according to these tests, you're dead! Nevertheless I notice that you can still hear. But that's no proof that you're alive either. Dead people probably hear what's going on, otherwise their relatives and friends wouldn't weep and bewail in their presence. Now tell me, are you hungry? You know, dead people don't eat."

"Oh, Reb Shloime!" Avrom sat up joyfully. "I'm

starved! Do you know when I had breakfast? Before dawn!"

"All right," said the scientist, "this is proof that you're not dead. Get up and have lunch! Did you bring your lunch with you?"

"Of course," answered Avrom. "It's in my pocket."

But Moishe the Miller interrupted. "No, Avrom, put your lunch away. My wife prepared a meal for all of you."

Well, Moishe's wife served a fine, plentiful meal. Everybody enjoyed the food but the Litvak foreman. He claimed that he had a terrific headache. Shloime the Scientist scoffed.

"The Litvaks are impossible. Avrom fell off the tree and the Litvak has a headache! There's no logic in anything they say or do."

The railroad comes to Helm

SOMETHING TREMENDOUS HAPPENED TO Helm! The Warsaw–Berlin railroad was extended almost to the heart of town, a mere three miles from the city. On the day the railroad was opened, the entire population of the town gathered at the railroad station to witness the great event.

On the shining rails stood ten red coaches. At their head was a panting engine, puffing smoke and steam. In the locomotive sat the engineer with his assistant, ready to start the train. At the door of the station house, the dispatcher waited beside a big bell, ready to give the signal.

Isaac the Wagoner stood amid a crowd of Helmites, his hands in his pockets, his legs spread apart. He spoke with a voice of authority.

"I don't care what all the scientists claim. I took a good look at the engine and there isn't even a loft for hay! There's not a sign of a horse. As an old wagoner, I say, 'No horses, no pulling! No pulling, no go!' "

The dispatcher gave the first signal. He rang the bell

once. Immediately the engineer pressed a lever and a puff of smoke arose from the locomotive's chimney. He pulled another handle and a billow of steam hissed forth. The engineer's assistant pulled a cord and a shrill sound pierced the air. But the engine stood still.

Isaac said triumphantly, "I told you—'No horses, no pulling out!' "

A minute later the dispatcher gave the second signal. The bell rang twice. Again the engineer pushed a handle. A bigger puff of smoke rushed from the chimney of the engine. More steam was forced with a great hiss from a side valve. Two shrill, piercing whistles split the air, but the train did not move.

"I told you!" Isaac jeered. " 'No horses, no pulling out!' Let them ring bells, blow whistles, puff steam! 'No horses, no go!' "

The dispatcher gave the third signal. A long, shrieking whistle rent the air and the train began to puff and huff, the wheels rolled, and before anybody knew how it had happened, the train had disappeared into the horizon.

Everybody stood agape. But Isaac the Wagoner was not perturbed.

"So it started! But they'll never be able to stop it. I say it won't work. 'No horses, no go.' "

But it did work. It seemed that they could start and stop the engine at will. Trains arrived twice a day, at twelve noon and at six in the evening, always on schedule

to the minute. The Helmites were both impressed and perturbed. "The world changes and we stand still."

They called a Town Meeting. As usual, Gimpel the Mayor was the chief speaker.

"My dear Helmites, until today we assumed that there is no wisdom outside of Helm, and we were right. We have with us a few Litvaks, and occasionally visitors come

from the outside world; and surely there is nothing to be excited about in their scholarship or wit. But we saw with our eyes what happened at the railroad station. The train did run, against all logic and reason. Ten coaches moved without a horse! Maybe it was magic, maybe it was science. One thing is certain: The world changes! Something is going on that we're not aware of.''

"So, what shall we do?" a voice called out.

"Years ago," answered Gimpel, "we found that the world looked upon us as fools. My father Mottel, may he rest in peace, was at that time mayor of the town. He decided to send someone to acquaint the world with our ways, and to observe theirs.

"I was chosen to be the emissary to the world. I spent years outside Helm, travelling far and wide. There was nothing to learn from the world. But I did find one nice custom: Every village and city kept a Town Record. We decided that Helm must have a Town Record, too. Ours must be the best in the world, for we record everything. Just yesterday we noted all that took place at the railroad station, including Isaac's opinion. Now, I suggest that we send three of our best citizens out into the world to observe what is going on today. I think they should visit Vilna, which is called the Jerusalem of Lithuania."

A decision like this cannot be made at one Town Meeting. The people of Helm prefer to deliberate and discuss, and consider the reasons for and against every suggestion.

Another six Town Meetings were called before they agreed to send a mission, with Shloime the Scientist as its head. The other two members were Reuben the Water-Carrier and Abba, the grandson of Gimpel the Mayor. Abba was being groomed as his grandfather's successor . . . a true Helmite.

The holes in the bagels

IN VILNA THE THREE EMISSARIES WENT directly to a fine hotel. The next day they called a conference and deliberated a long time before they decided on a plan. They would divide the city into three sections. Each of them would explore one section thoroughly. After seven days they would meet again in the hotel to talk over their findings.

So they did. On the seventh day, the three Helmites reassembled as planned, and sat down to their business. First spoke Abba, Mayor Gimpel's grandson.

"Brethren, there is nothing to learn from the people of Vilna. One is more stupid than the other. Worst of all, they have no sense of humor. As I wandered through the city, all I found was noise, hurry and bustle. There is not a shred of reason or logic in their behavior. In the market place I saw a coachman talking to a group of men—coachmen and wagoners, I suppose. He was boasting about a horse he had bought from a Gypsy.

" 'The horse is so fast,' he bragged, 'that if you start

from Vilna at twelve o'clock at night, you arrive in Ash-ashok at three in the morning.'

"'You're a liar!' someone called out. 'The son and grandson of a bragger! It's more than twenty-eight miles from Vilna to Ashashok. No horse can run that fast.'

"'Who's a liar and a braggart, me? I should bust you in the nose for that! But I don't want to dirty my hand with your blood and snot. I tell you, if I leave Vilna right after the midnight train, I'll reach Ashashok by 3 A.M. I can prove it to you. Be one of my passengers.'

"Then I intervened.

"Wait a moment! I assume you're telling the truth, and that you'll arrive in Ashashok at three in the morning. But what will you do there so early before dawn?

"They all looked at me and burst out laughing. 'I'll bet my shirt you're a Helmite!' somebody yelled.

"'Of course,' I answered, irritated. 'I'm a Helmite. But you didn't answer my question.'

"Well, they began laughing more and I left them there, shaking with foolish mirth. Do you see anything funny in what I asked?"

"I had a similar experience," Reuben reported. "I passed a capmaker's shop—you know how they display their wares in big windows there. There was one cap I liked very much. I stopped to look at it, and the owner invited me into the shop. He was very friendly and polite and asked me which cap I liked. I pointed it out to him.

'Why don't you buy it?' he asked. 'It's not expensive.' I told him, 'I'd like to buy it, but I'm embarrassed. I thought I had the measure of my head in my pocket, but I searched everywhere and can't find it. I must have left it in Helm.'

38

"Well, the shopkeeper called in all the help and asked me to repeat what I had said. I did, and you've never heard such boisterous hilarity in your whole life! I stood there and found myself wondering what all these fools of Vilna were laughing at."

Here, Shloime picked up the story.

"The trouble with you is that you talk to the people of Vilna as if they were rational, like the Helmites. I know the world better than you. I've even visited Warsaw. Therefore, I listen, even if I don't agree. I never argue. Sometimes I'm ready to scream out: Fools, idiots and imbeciles! But, I hold my tongue. What's the use of arguing with fools? Listen to this. I was standing in a bakeshop, looking at something I liked. Then I heard a man say to a friend, 'Do you remember Benjamin, the son of Leibke the Shoemaker, who left Vilna fifteen years ago? He emigrated to London. Well, he left Vilna in a single pair of old, torn pants. Now, he has a million!'

" 'You don't say, a cool million!'

" 'His father told me.'

"The other man clucked his tongue. 'Some people are lucky!'

"I looked at them. What is there to envy, I ask you? The emigrant left with one pair of old, torn trousers and now he has a million old, torn pants. What will he do with a million torn and worthless pants? But I kept my peace. What's the sense of arguing with your inferiors? Besides, I was fascinated with what I saw in the bakery. I discovered something worth taking home. Look, I brought you some."

Shloime opened a large bag and took out a bunch of baked rings.

"What are those?" asked the others.

"They're called bagels."

"Bagels? That's a new one," said Abba.

"New or old," answered Shloime, "what difference does it make? Look at them! Did you ever see baked goods like this? It's shaped like a millstone, with a hole in the middle and a ring of dough around the hole. But never mind the shape. Taste it! I have been young now I am old, but I have never eaten anything as delicious as this. I say, taste it!"

They sampled the bagels. They smacked their lips and admitted that Shloime was right. They made a whole meal of bagels with milk, devouring a half-dozen bagels and three glasses of milk apiece.

The next day, all three of them hurried to the bakery. They each ate a dozen bagels, fresh from the oven, and found them still better warm and crisp. When they could

eat no more, they said to the baker, "Please, baker, teach us how to bake bagels. We'll pay you handsomely for your trouble."

The baker agreed. He showed them how to knead the dough and how to cook the bagels in a big iron kettle, filled with boiling water. Then he taught them how to put the boiled bagels on the baker's peel and bake them on the floor of a hot brick oven.

They watched carefully, and then Reuben turned to Shloime, "I didn't grasp everything. Do you understand how to bake them?"

"I think so, but I'd like the baker to go over it again, from the beginning. Especially, I'd like to know how he gets the hole in the middle."

The baker looked at them, and then asked, quietly, "Are you from Helm, my brother Jews?"

They nodded.

"If that's the case, there's no point in going over the whole thing again. You surely grasped it all. As for the round hole in the center, that's simple. You take a ready-made hole, surround it with dough, join the ends, and there you have a bagel, ready to bake!"

Shloime was a bit ruffled. "Reb baker, I understood that the first time! My question is, where do you get the round holes?"

"Oh, that, my dear Helmites!" answered the baker. "I inherited a supply of round holes from my father. He inherited them from his father. I'm descended from generations and generations of bagel bakers, as far as . . . maybe as far back as our father Abraham. But as for your supply . . . Wait, let me look you over." He surveyed them. "You're sturdy fellows. You each can carry six strings of bagels on your neck, three dozen to a string. Eighteen dozen apiece comes to fifty-four dozen bagels. Fifty-four dozen bagels means six hundred and forty-

eight holes. So you have a goodly supply of round holes from Vilna. All you have to do is be careful to leave the hole intact when you eat the bagel, so it can be used again. If you sell a bagel, tell the customer not to destroy the hole. That way you'll have an endless supply of round holes."

Right then and there, the three Helmites decided to return home. Each one put six ropes of bagels around his neck, like necklaces. They stuffed as many bagels as they could into their pockets, to eat on the road.

It's quite a distance from Vilna to Helm. They walked a day, rested a night, walked another day and rested another night . . . for five full days. On the sixth day, as they approached Helm, the country became hilly, and walking was more difficult. Two miles from Helm, they climbed a steep hill. Below it, lay a village. Tired and perspiring, they sat down. After a while, Shloime spoke.

"Abba and Reuben, don't be in a hurry to carry the bagels on your necks. Do you remember when we built our synagogue and couldn't carry the great oak log down the hill? We were told that any round object can be rolled down a hill. Do you remember?"

"Of course, we remember!"

"Then, why carry ropes of bagels around our necks? Aren't bagels round? Let's take the bagels off the ropes, which are chafing our necks badly, and roll them down the hill!"

"That's a wonderful idea! Shloime, you have a head on your shoulders!"

They removed the ropes of bagels from their necks, untied the strings, and rolled the bagels down the hill.

But no sooner did the bagels reach the valley than dogs and pigs from the village rushed out and made short work of them. When the Helmites saw what was happening, they shouted, "All right; eat all you want—but be careful with the holes! Watch out for the holes!"

But dogs are dogs, and pigs are pigs . . . when are they considerate? By the time the Helmites reached the foot of the hill, there was not a sign of a bagel, nor a trace of a round hole. Dogs are dogs and pigs are pigs . . . they have no idea of values.

Well, Shloime did not give in. He sat in seclusion for seven weeks. He thought and figured, figured and thought, and with the help of a compass made circles on a baker's board. Then he showed the bakers how to ring the holes with dough. It took them a long time to learn to bake bagels without ready-made holes, but they managed.

Mayor Gimpel's golden shoes

THE RAILROAD BROUGHT A RESTLESSNESS TO Helm. It started with Gimpel, who was not only the richest man in Helm, but a descendant of its first settler. He was a Helmite: the son, the grandson, and the great, great grandson of a Helmite! Besides all that, or because of it, he had been mayor for fifteen years.

He called a Town Meeting and laid a grievance before the open assembly.

"I have been mayor of our city for fifteen years. When we have a Town Meeting I sit at the head of the table, so everybody knows I'm mayor and pays me the proper respect. But when I walk in the street, I'm dressed like anybody else and nobody recognizes me. No one gives me the honor due me, not even the children. At the railroad station every official wears a uniform to show his rank. Even the lowliest has a cockade on his hat. But look at me! Do I have anything to signify my station and importance? I demand a uniform fitting to my high office!"

Everybody agreed that Gimpel was right. But what

insignia should he be given? They discussed and argued, they reasoned and debated, and came to no conclusion. They couldn't imitate the uniforms of the Gentile officials. Isn't it written, "Neither shall ye walk in their statutes?" And what uniforms are there besides those of the Gentile officials?

After discussing this for seven nights, it was decided to turn the question over to a committee of three: Shloime the Scientist, Pinya the Philosopher, and Berel the Beadle. They were given seven weeks to study the matter and bring in a report.

At the end of seven weeks, a Town Meeting was called and Shloime read the committee's recommendation.

"We have thought over the problem carefully. We can't recommend a fine satin *kaftan* for the mayor, for this is the garment which distinguishes the Rabbi of the town. We don't want people to confuse the two. The Rabbi is honored for his Torah, for his learning, and Gimpel demands *kovod*, honor for his wealth and station. These are different kinds of honor.

"Neither can we recommend a fine fur hat with twelve tails, for that is the distinction of a Chasidic Rabbi— the badge of Holiness. We don't want anyone to confuse the mayor with the Chasidic Rabbi. The Rabbi is of holy stock, but Gimpel is only rich and famous. Therefore, we recommend a pair of golden shoes for our mayor. When he wears them, everybody will know that he is

Gimpel, different from everybody else, the mayor of the town, to whom respect is due."

The people acclaimed the recommendation.

In two weeks, the shoes were ready. Gimpel the Mayor put them on and went for a stroll. That self-same evening he called a Town Meeting.

"I don't want to belittle, God forbid, the labor and the merit of the distinguished committee," he announced. "They meant well. The idea would probably work in Warsaw, where the streets are paved and washed every day. But here, in Helm! Our city is at the foot of the mountain. The streets are muddy in the spring and autumn, dusty in the summer, and wet with snow in the winter. I took a short stroll today. Before I had gone twenty steps, the shoes became muddy! Even the goldsmith would not have known that I wore his golden shoes. Therefore, no one recognized me and no one paid me honor. In the summer the shoes will get dusty; in the autumn they will be muddy, and in the winter they will be covered with snow. So what good do they do me?"

Shloime the Scientist was calm. "This is easily remedied. We'll order a pair of leather overshoes. You'll wear them over the golden shoes, to protect them from becoming muddy."

"An excellent idea!" the whole of Helm cried. "Excellent!" repeated the elders seated about the table.

No sooner said than done! Gimpel put leather over-

shoes on the golden shoes and strolled in the muddy streets of Helm. The same day he called a Town Meeting.

"Now, what's the trouble?" wondered the burghers of Helm.

Well, there was trouble, indeed!

"True, my dear Helmites, the overshoes did protect the golden shoes from mud," Gimpel complained. "But they also covered their glitter, so that no one recognized me or paid me honor."

This was a knotty problem. The Helmites sat in council for seven days and seven nights. Finally, they hit upon an idea. The shoemaker would make holes in the overshoes so that the gold would show through, and everybody would know who the wearer was.

But it didn't work again! A Town Meeting had to be called the same day that Gimpel ventured out with the perforated overshoes. He explained, "True, when I put on the overshoes with the little round holes at home, the gold shone and glistened very impressively. But no sooner did I go out to the street . . . well, nothing prevented the mud from going through the holes! No one saw the gold. No one knew that I was Gimpel the Mayor, and nobody paid me any honor."

Now the Helmites began to think in earnest. This required real thought. After seven days and nights, a solution was offered by Reuben the Water-Carrier, the rising star of Helm.

"Let's stuff the holes in the overshoes with straw. That will prevent the mud from getting on the shoes."

"It's an idea," they all agreed. "But it has a big defect. The straw will also cover the glitter of the gold." Reuben argued that this might be so, but everybody who saw the overshoes with holes stuffed with straw would suspect that there was something behind the overshoes.

The Helmites thought differently. People might take Gimpel for a common pauper who wore shoes with holes stuffed with straw to keep his feet dry. Then Abba, the Mayor's grandson, came up with a brilliant idea.

"My grandfather, the mayor, should go back to his ordinary leather shoes and, over them, the overshoes with the holes stuffed with straw. But, so that people won't mistake him for a pauper, he should also wear the golden shoes—not on his feet, but on his hands—the left shoe on his left hand and the right shoe on his right hand. The golden shoes will never get dirty. People will see the shining gold and will know that he's Gimpel, the mayor of the town, and they'll give him his due honor."

If you ever go to Helm, and see a man walking in torn shoes, the holes stuffed with straw, you might suspect that he is the mayor of the town who neglected to put the golden shoes on his hands. He left them at home, where his wife guards them.

The dedication
of the cemetery

WHEN THE TUMULT OF THE GOLDEN SHOES had quieted down, a new problem arose. Zundel, the chief trustee of the Holy Association of the Burial Society, who had complete charge of the cemetery, came to the mayor in alarm. He reported that the cemetery, which was God knows how old, was practically filled. New burial grounds had to be dedicated in a hurry.

A Town Meeting was immediately called. The elders sat about a round table while the rest of the townspeople stood in the hall. Gimpel put the golden shoes near him, to mark the head of the table, and the debate began.

All agreed that new burial grounds must be dedicated. The question was, where? The young generation held that the new cemetery should be located on top of the hill, beside the watermill which is now a treadmill. It's a nice spot and the dead would have a beautiful view. Behind the cemetery is a thick forest where thousands of birds nest. Their singing would fall sweetly on the ears of the dead and gladden their hearts. To the left stretch

wide fields and meadows. The soft winds would cool the dead in the summer, when the sun beats mercilessly on the graves. From the front of the cemetery the whole town of Helm could be seen by the dead, so they could keep an eye on it and protect it.

51

But the older people argued, "True, the top of the hill is a beautiful spot. But every family has at least one member resting in the old cemetery. When the month of Elul arrives and we must visit the graves to pay respect to the dead, it will be a great hardship. First we must prostrate ourselves on the graves of our beloved in the old cemetery, and then, after a good cry, which wrecks every bone and muscle, we'll have to climb the hill to the new cemetery. No, it's impractical! The new cemetery must be near the old one."

The older generation won. The Town Meeting was ready to close when Reuben, the rising sage, arose.

"People of Helm, now we must determine the area of the new burial ground. We have to fence off the Holy Grounds to keep out goats and cows. We must know beforehand how much lumber to buy and how many stakes to prepare."

Right then and there it was decided to call another Town Meeting.

No one had the slightest idea what the length and breadth of the new cemetery should be. True, they could take the old one as a guide, but it had been dedi-

cated when Helm was a village, whereas it is now a "mother city" among the cities of Israel and still keeps growing. The size of the new cemetery could not be solved in a hurry.

They met for seven consecutive nights. On the eighth, Abba, the grandson of Gimpel the Mayor, came up with a sagacious idea.

"All of us, but all of us—men and women, old and young, children, even babes in arms—must go to the field and lie down, near one another, flat on the ground. Of course, the men and women will lie separately, and the children in the special children's section. It's not necessary to specify that the learned and the important burghers shall stretch themselves on the ground at the front rows of the graves and the plain people in the back rows. We also should allot a goodly plot for transients. Then Shloime the Mathematician can measure the whole area. And that is that!" finished Abba, triumphantly.

It was so logical that the whole assembly rose to cheer. Everybody, that is, but Shloime the Mathematician.

"Wait a while! Don't cheer yet!"

"Why, Shloime! Isn't it a sensible solution?"

"Of course! It's a beautiful idea. But Abba forgot something very important."

"What's that?"

"Well," Shloime spoke slowly, "it's well known that when people get older they gain weight. Some get very

bulky. If we measure the cemetery to the size we are now, it will be filled before you wink."

Now Gimpel the Mayor came to the rescue. There is nothing like old wine for taste and an old Helmite for ideas!

"I'm glad Shloime called our attention to that important problem. But it can be surmounted very easily. We'll all get dressed in our winter clothes—winter underwear, suits with padded linings and, over all that, our overcoats. Those who have fur coats should wear them. These heavy clothes will make us bulky and will compensate for the weight we'll gain as we get older."

So, on a nice, hot summer day, all Helm—men, women, children and infants—bundled up in heavy woolen underwear, in suits and dresses with thickly padded linings and, on top of all that, heavy winter overcoats. They trudged to the new cemetery, sweating and chafing. All stretched themselves out on the ground as prearranged—men and women separately, children in the youth section, infants in a corner, and the learned and the important burghers in front. Shloime measured off the area, including a plot for himself, and drove stakes into the ground as markers for its boundaries.

To reward Abba for his brilliant idea it was resolved, at a special Town Meeting, that he should have the honor of being the first person buried in the new cemetery.

Whether it turned out so, I do not know.

The great calamity
and if

ON A HILL AT THE EDGE OF THE TOWN THERE stands the hut where Shmuel the Shingle-Maker lives with his wife Dwashe and their daughter Teltza. Shmuel and Dwashe have only one child—but what a one! She is a real beauty, with deep brown eyes, long black hair and skin like the pale pink petals of a rose. The Helmites say, her forehead is high and round because she has so much brains.

Yes, she is clever and full of the wisdom of Helm. It was Teltza who proved that the moon isn't made of cheese. She pointed to it swimming in the river, and observed shrewdly, "If the moon were made of cheese, as you say, wouldn't it melt in the water?"

She doesn't take anything for granted. Once her parents were invited to the wedding of a leading citizen of Helm. They were overjoyed at the honor, but even more so at the prospect of a wonderful meal: stuffed fish, chicken and *kishke*, *tzimes* and chicken noodle soup, wines and liquors, and the cakes, tarts, almonds and raisins.

As they were ready to leave for the gala occasion, Dwashe remarked to Shmuel, "Tonight's going to be the most wonderful night of our lives!"

When they returned at dawn, they found Teltza sitting at an open window, looking out at the sky and the fields.

"Teltza, why aren't you asleep?" they asked her in astonishment.

Teltza's voice was disappointed. "You said tonight would be the most wonderful night of your lives. Well, I've been watching since you left. It was a night like any other night."

Then there is the time Teltza and her cousin visited their grandmother, who gave them each five cookies. Teltza quickly ate her five; but the other girl, who was younger, could eat only three.

Teltza, who had an eye on the remaining cookies, asked, "Rachel, why don't you eat the other two cookies?"

"I wish I could," sighed her cousin, "but I'm full. I ate three already."

"You were foolish," Teltza pointed out. "Why didn't you eat these two first?"

Yes, she had the wisdom of Helm!

One beautiful spring morning, Teltza was doing her chores. She opened the window to let in the fresh spring breeze from the fields. Below her, the town of Helm was spread out, serene and beautiful in the morning haze. Teltza surveyed it contentedly.

"I was born here, in this wonderful town," she mused. "My father and mother, and their fathers and mothers before them, were all born here. Everybody in town knows me. My uncles, aunts and cousins all tell me I'm beautiful. Papa and Mama, Grandpa and Grandma surely love me. Now Mama has made me a new Sabbath dress of flowered gingham, and I'm as happy as that robin chirping in the tree!"

Teltza sang as she swept her step light. After a while she leaned on the broom and mused further.

"I'm fifteen now. In a year or two, Papa will find me a fine young scholar. We'll be engaged for six months and then we'll have the wedding. It will be a big, beautiful affair, with dancing, merry-making and great rejoicing."

She sang louder, sweeping in time to her song. Then she paused again.

"A year after the wedding, I'll give birth to a boy. When my husband makes the *brith*, the whole town will envy me! But that won't be anything compared to my son's Bar Mitzvah celebration! By that time my husband will be rich, and he'll make a feast—two feasts: one, the day before, for the beggars, and then a sumptuous one for the relatives and friends—and . . ." She broke off abruptly. "Oh, God!"

Now the words came rapidly. "What if he cries out, like the son of the great lady Shunammite in the Bible, 'My head, my head!' and dies!"

She dropped the broom and wrung her hands.

"What a calamity! I won't be able to stand it! True, my parents will bemoan my misfortune. So will my grandfather and grandmother. But even my parents will not mourn for more than six months. They will be comforted by their other grandchildren. My favorite aunt, Beile, will also mourn and cry for a couple of days; then she'll stop. After all, she can't cry forever. Aunt Breine will grieve for a day only. She doesn't like me too much. But I, the mother, will not outlive the calamity! I will die of distress. They'll bury me near my darling son, and then there will be two fresh mounds in the cemetery of Helm. People from fifty miles around will hear of it and weep!"

Teltza began to moan and wail.

"Woe is me! Why am I so unfortunate as to lose my boy at Bar Mitzvah and pass away before I'm thirty? Two young trees uprooted! Two rosebushes cut off in full bloom! Rivers of tears should be shed at such a calamity!"

And she began to bawl at the top of her lungs.

Teltza's mother heard the outburst and ran into the room, distraught. "What happened?"

Teltza was crying so hard that she couldn't speak. She could only wring her hands and wail louder. At this, her mother began to shriek.

Teltza's grandmother, who lived nearby, heard the shrieking and wailing, and ran to the house to see what

had happened. There she found Teltza and her mother, both crying and wringing their hands.

"Two mounds in the cemetery!" Teltza bawled.

At these words, the grandmother began to wring her hands and emit piercing screams.

The commotion could be heard throughout the neighborhood. Neighbors came running, and when they saw the three women howling, they knew that something terrible had happened. They joined in bewailing the calamity which had befallen the beautiful Teltza and her mother and grandmother.

Word spread quickly. Aunts, uncles and cousins streamed to the house. Nobody knew what had happened, but obviously it was something dreadful. They all joined in the crying.

Soon the courtyard was black with people, all wailing, lamenting and wringing their hands.

Finally, the Rabbi of Helm arrived. When he saw everyone crying and moaning, he realized that a great calamity had befallen somebody. In such an event there is only one thing to do. He called out, "Jews of Helm, why are you standing idly in the face of such a disaster? Let us chant Psalms."

The whole congregation started to chant Psalms, right from the first chapter. "Happy is the man that hath not walked in the counsel of the wicked, nor stood in the way of sinners, nor sat in the seat of the scornful. . . ."

The wailing and chanting reached Moishe Litvak in the mill. Usually Moishe does not become alarmed at anything that goes on in Helm. But this time he became frightened—a whole congregation lamenting! He started on a run towards Shmuel's house, but as he approached he saw no sign of trouble. Nothing appeared to be amiss.

Amid the throng in the courtyard he spotted Berel the Beadle, who is not exactly a Helmite. Berel's eyes were dry and he did not sway and chant Psalms.

"Berel, what's going on here?" Moishe asked.

"Some are crying, and some are wailing, and they all chant Psalms."

"But what happened?"

"I don't know. Ask one of the family."

Moishe stopped a plump woman. "Auntie, what happened? What's the crying about?"

"You heartless Litvak!" she greeted him. "See how calm and dry-eyed he is! Questions, he asks—that's all he has on his mind! Look at Teltza, her mother, her old grandmother! A heart of stone could melt!"

"But what happened?"

"How should I know?"

Moishe tried to talk to the grandmother, and the mother, and finally, Teltza herself.

"Listen, Teltza, stop your bawling for a minute and tell me what the trouble is. Maybe I can help."

"Moishe Litvak, he's beyond help!"

"Who's beyond help?"

"My son! My darling who just became Bar Mitzvah. He died!"

Moishe is seldom surprised at anything a Helmite does, but now he was taken aback.

"Your *son*?"

"Of course, my son! Why else would I cry so bitterly?"

Now Moishe came to himself. He didn't laugh. He talked to Teltza in dead earnest.

"Listen, Teltza, you're only fifteen and you're not even married. So how can you have a son thirteen years old?"

"True, Reb Moishe," she answered, the tears flowing. "But suppose I were older and married. I'd be about thirty when my son was Bar Mitzvah. If he called out, like the son of the great lady Shunammite in the Bible and died suddenly, wouldn't it be a calamity?"

Moishe controlled himself, and kept a straight face. He did what a Helmite would have done: He used logic.

"Teltza, yes, it would be a great calamity, *if* you were married, and *if* you had a son, and *if* he got sick on the eve of the Bar Mitzvah, and *if* he died. You see, there are four '*if*'s.' But not a single 'if' came to pass: You're not married, you don't have a son, he didn't take sick, and he didn't die. So Teltza, there's nothing to cry about."

The clever Teltza looked at him, her eyes wide. "Reb Moishe, I never thought of that! You're right!"

She stopped crying. When Teltza stopped crying, her

mother and grandmother shut their mouths. Before you could wink an eye, everybody had stopped.

When the wailing ceased, the Rabbi left off chanting Psalms, whereupon everyone else called a halt. The Rabbi took a snuff of tobacco, sneezed heartily, and everybody chorused, *"Gezundheit!"*

Said the Rabbi, "You see, my dear Jews, nothing helps more in time of distress than the chanting of a few Psalms. It's a sure remedy. You saw with your own eyes how it helped Teltza!"

62

Yossel-Zissel the Melamed

YOSSEL-ZISSEL THE CHUMOSH-MELAMED, teacher of the Pentateuch, was a little fellow, narrow in the shoulders, but wiry and strong, with prominent cheek bones and fiery dark eyes. Parents liked him, for he did his work honestly and efficiently, and because he imbued the children with the true spirit of Helm. But above all, they appreciated him for the ability of being a good disciplinarian.

In those days, all over the world, teachers used corporal punishment. Whipping a child to discipline him was part of the curriculum. A school was equipped with textbooks, slates, slate pencils, a blackboard perhaps, a pointer, and a fine birch rod close at the teacher's right hand. Helm was no exception.

Yossel-Zissel was considered a disciplinarian among disciplinarians. Every unruly boy, every troublesome and rebellious youngster, eventually landed in his *cheder*, the school of teaching Chumosh, Talmud, including Jewish customs, laws, ethics, and moral behavior.

When a child was brought to him, the first thing Yossel-Zissel did was to point to a great tablet hanging on the wall. On it was printed a verse from Proverbs. Yossel-Zissel would make the new boy read it aloud.

"Foolishness is always in the heart of a child, but the rod of correction shall drive it out of him."

Then Yossel-Zissel would add, "You should know that I strictly observe this verse and I enforce it because it's true; isn't it written in the Holy Scriptures? So, try to be good! No, you won't escape chastisement entirely, because it is written in the Holy Bible: 'There is not a righteous man upon the earth that does always good and does not sin.' And you're not a righteous man, as far as I've heard. You're unruly, troublesome and stubborn. So, beware! Try to behave, and you'll be punished with compassion."

Often, parents with an only son who was difficult packed him off to Yossel-Zissel's *cheder*. The mother usually came to Yossel-Zissel on the sly, without her husband's knowledge, and pleaded, "Please, Rebbe, go easy with the boy! Deal gently with the child, for my sake. He is my one and only eye."

Yossel-Zissel would boom at her, sternly, "Do you love your son or not?"

"Of course, I love him," stammered the mother.

"Then why do you tell me to withhold just punishment from him? Isn't it written: 'He who spares his rod hates

his son, but he who loves him seeks to discipline him'?
Begone, woman! Go to your pots and pans, and leave the
education of your son to wiser people than you."

In spite of his harsh discipline, Yossel-Zissel was liked

by most of the children. They appreciated that, severe though he was when a child deserved punishment, he could also be sentimental and warm. The dusk hour was usually set apart for storytelling. And on Saturday afternoons and the half-holidays, Yossel-Zissel sat and talked with them as if they were his equals.

Not only did he tell them stories from the Midrash and Talmud and miraculous tales of the holy Chasidic rabbis, but he also discussed worldly matters and explained things that puzzled them. And the children of Helm were curious and full of questions like children all over the world.

When the government opened a telegraph office in the railroad station, the pupils were puzzled. "Who needs a telegraph office and how does it work?"

Yossel-Zissel explained everything.

"The government needs it. A telegraph office is a *must* for the Czar. The Russian Empire is big, very big, and the ruler is always afraid of rebellion and trouble. So, every morning he sends telegrams to all the stations: 'Is all well in your town?' In olden times he had to send couriers, but now he gets an answer by wire in an hour: 'All's well!' If there's rebellion, the telegraph operator answers one word: 'Trouble!' The operator is sparing with words, because each word costs money."

"But, Rebbe, the capital is hundreds and hundreds of miles away! How does the telegraph carry the words?"

"Well, they stretch wires from the capital to, say, our

city. When they want to send a telegram they pinch, or twist the wire in a certain manner at the capital. The wire at our end then turns in the same manner. Each twist or turn means a definite letter. How's it possible to get an immediate response from such a distance, at the other end of the wire? Well, that shouldn't surprise you. You've seen big dogs. It may be several feet from the tip of a dog's tail to his mouth. Still, as soon as you twist his tail, his mouth begins to bark.''

Yossel-Zissel never lacked an answer. Sometimes the boys asked ethical questions.

"Rebbe, suppose you found a pocketbook with fifty thousand rubles. Would you return it?"

"Well," answered Yossel-Zissel, "I'll be honest with you. I'd inquire very carefully as to who lost the money. If a rich man lost it, say a Rothschild, I'd ask for a reward. But if a poor man had lost it, say a man like Reuben the Water-Carrier, who hasn't a shirt to his back, I'd return it immediately, to the last kopeck! I wouldn't take a reward even if it were offered! Who wants to take money from a pauper?"

There is another favorite story of Yossel-Zissel's great knowledge and insight.

When the children studied the Biblical story of the giant Og, King of Bashan, they came to the verse: "For only Og, King of Bashan, remained of the remnant of the giants." "How tall was the giant, Og?" they asked.

Yossel-Zissel answered, "It's hard to say. We don't know the kind of measurements they used at that time. But I can give you an inkling. Once, on a Purim, Og went for a walk. It was a wet, rainy day. Sleet, mixed with rain, descended from the sky. Well, Og's feet got wet and he caught a cold. But he didn't get a running nose until the last day of Pesach! It took five weeks for the cold to travel from Og's feet to his head. That's how tall he was!"

And as the children still looked bewildered and puzzled, Yossel-Zissel nudged them: "Why do you look so puzzled? Doesn't my answer give you a fairly good idea of how tall he was?" "Yes it does," the children answered. "But Rebbe, why didn't he buy rubber boots?" Yossel-Zissel paused for a moment, then said: "There were no boots big enough in any store for a giant like Og!"

Because of a blintz

69

YOSSEL-ZISSEL WASN'T EVEN A LESSER LIGHT in Helm. Still, there are fourteen closely written pages about him in the Town Record—all because Yossel-Zissel loved blintzes. It seems he once tasted a blintz and fell in love with it! As a result, he had two great adventures.

Here's the story that is told in the Town Record.

In their young days, before the children were grown, Yossel-Zissel and his wife Sossie had a struggle to feed the family. When the *melamed* was thirty years old, he was the father of nine children—the oldest eleven, and the youngest an infant in arms.

Yossel-Zissel had as many pupils as his *cheder* could accommodate, but still he did not earn enough to provide his family with the absolute necessities. Tuition was small, and not every parent paid in full at the end of the season. So there were frequent meatless Sabbaths and even Sabbaths without *challeh*.

To support the family, Sossie knitted socks for the well-to-do; but her earnings, claimed Yossel-Zissel, were just enough for water in the soup. She, however, explained that taking care of nine children, a house and a husband was more than enough for one woman and left little time for knitting.

Yossel-Zissel's great ambition was to own a goat. If he owned a goat, he said, his troubles would disappear like smoke on a windy day, like a nightmare on a bright morning. There would be milk for the children, and perhaps cheese, cream and butter. There might even be milk to sell, so that one might see a silver coin.

This is what Yossel-Zissel said out loud. But deep in his heart he had a secret—a different reason why he wanted a goat. But his heart didn't dare tell it to his mouth—what was he, a glutton? The truth was that he wanted a goat because he always dreamed about blintzes.

Ah, blintzes! Not only had he heard about their wonderful taste, but once he had actually sampled it!

One Shavuoth he had been invited into the house of a pupil whose father wanted to hear his son read the week's portion of the Pentateuch. Afterwards Yossel-Zissel was treated to two blintzes, the delicacy for Shavuoth, the holiday on which dairy dishes are served.

Their very look threw him into raptures! The dough was yellow with eggs. The cheese was glossy and rich from all the butter, and both blintzes swam in a pool of

cream. To top it, the hostess sprinkled it all with cinnamon and sugar.

Yossel-Zissel ate the blintzes slowly, but they were gone before he could taste them properly. These two blintzes were just enough to arouse a great hunger in him—a passionate desire to be sated with that delicacy.

One night he dreamed that he was at the table with his wife and children. Sossie said to him in a mysterious voice, "Now, my Yossel-Zissel, I have a treat for you!"

She brought out a deep bowl heaped with blintzes. Well, everyone ate to his heart's content, but at the end of the meal two blintzes remained in the bowl, swimming in rich cream. Yossel-Zissel put the two blintzes on his plate. "Yossel-Zissel," Sossie scolded, "I don't begrudge you the blintzes, but do you know how many you had? A full dozen! You'll get sick!"

Yossel-Zissel smiled. She wasn't exactly right . . . he'd had fourteen. "No one can ever have his fill of blintzes," he answered. "They're light as down. Who ever got sick from blintzes?"

Then he awoke. There was such an emptiness and hunger in his stomach! It was a longing for one thing only—a blintz!

In the still of the night, he lay with open eyes, his mind revolving like a windmill. He had to find a way to have blintzes! Finally, he hit on it!

The next morning he told his wife, "Sossie, dear, I

work hard, but you work harder. You nurse a child, take care of the house and the children. You cook, bake and mend. Added to all that, you earn a coin here and there from your knitting. Yet in spite of both our earnings, there's seldom enough left for shoes or clothes. But if we had our own goat!"

Sossie looked at him, surprised, and said mockingly, "If and if! If my grandmother had four wheels she'd be a wagon! And if you were Gimpel the Mayor, you'd own a cow. And if you were the stationmaster, you'd have two cows and four dogs."

"Who needs four dogs? For that matter, who wants a dog altogether?"

"Don't interrupt!" said Sossie, irritated. "Let me finish! No, I'm not greedy either. I don't want Gimpel's cow. I'd be satisfied with a goat . . . any goat, black, white or brown, speckled or streaked. But where will you get the money for a goat? What good is the pepper when there is no fish? No chickens, no eggs; no eggs, no chicks. If we had the . . ."

"Will you turn off the faucet for a minute? I have a plan. Listen! Do you remember the trunk on wheels your father gave us as part of your dowry?"

Her eyes opened with amazement.

"Yes, I know we have a big trunk on wheels. Do you want to sell it? Who in Helm doesn't own a trunk like that?"

"No, no, I don't want to sell it. But listen—we should begin to save money every day . . ."

"Save from what? From the best carp you can't get more than one head. The fattest ox has only one skin. You earn just enough for the groats of the soup and I for the water."

Yossel-Zissel sighed.

"You're as full of proverbs and witticisms as a thistle is with thorns. I know we're poor, but still we can each save one kopeck a day. Imagine that you earn one kopeck less from your knitting. As for me, I'll save from my smoking. In a year we'll have over five rubles. That's enough for half a goat. In the middle of the next year we'll have about eight rubles. The rest we can borrow from the money lender. The goat's milk will pay for the weekly installments."

"Every day a kopeck? That's six kopecks a week . . . the cost of a loaf of bread and half a herring."

"I know, Sossie, it will be hard," Yossel-Zissel wheedled. "But the happiness it brings will be worth it. Listen! Do you like blintzes?"

"I hate them," she mocked. "Like a cat hates cream, like a rich man hates gold."

"Well, then," Yossel-Zissel remarked casually, "we'll ease up a little next Shavuoth. For the holiday we'll compromise. We'll open the trunk and take fifty or seventy-five kopecks to buy eggs, flour, milk, butter and cream. And you'll make blintzes for the holiday."

At that, Sossie smiled to herself, wryly.

"Agreed. How do we go about it?"

"It's simple. The trunk is empty. We'll make two slits on the lid—one on the right side and one on the left. Each day I'll drop a kopeck in the right slit and you in the left. We'll put two locks on the trunk. You'll have one key, and I'll have the other. Neither of us will be able to open the trunk without the other. Just before Shavuoth we'll open it Do you agree?"

"Agreed. When do we start?"

"Right now!" Yossel-Zissel was delighted. The trick had worked!

No sooner said than done! Yossel-Zissel made the slits and locked the trunk. Then he dropped a kopeck through the right slit and Sossie put one in the left slit. And that was that.

From the beginning Sossie had not intended to keep her part of the bargain. She knew she couldn't save six kopecks a week; and besides, she had caught on right away that Yossel-Zissel only wanted to accumulate enough for blintzes for Shavuoth. Her earnings were meager, and six kopecks could buy a bit of butter, a few glasses of milk and a full quart of whey, which is a delicious, refreshing drink. With the housework, and the knitting, and the nursing of the infant, she needed an occasional luxury to give her strength.

Yossel-Zissel, on the other hand, thought he had fooled Sossie. He can't get along without smoking. It's his only relaxation and pleasure. If he didn't light a cigarette now and then, he'd collapse from the noise and the carrying on of the twenty boys. The very thought of giving up smoking made him nervous! But she, Sossie . . . a kopeck a day wouldn't make any difference to her. At the end of a year there would be more than enough for real blintzes. Of course, she'd be angry when she found out he had cheated. Well, she'd get over it!

The year passed. The day before Shavuoth they opened the trunk. There was one kopeck to the right and one kopeck to the left . . . both coins covered with a year of dust.

The first to find his voice was Yossel-Zissel.

"You cheat! You never did put in more than the first kopeck!"

Sossie stood defiantly, her hand on her waist.

"Look who's accusing me! I, a nursing mother, should be deprived of the bare necessities so he can have blintzes for Shavuoth! If you hadn't cheated there'd be enough to eat blintzes till they came out of your nose! You didn't need my few kopecks!"

Yossel-Zissel saw red. His dream of blintzes for Shavuoth was gone. He raised his two fists, shrieking, "You! You dare scold me? I never have a moment's respite from you, from my pupils and from the children, I'll . . ."

Sossie's eyes blazed. "What? You raise a hand to me!"

I'm reluctant to tell it; but the truth is the truth. She seized his beard and he grabbed her wig, and they began to fight and struggle; to pull and push, till . . . the trunk stood open . . . Sossie lost her balance and fell in . . . pulling Yossel-Zissel after her. The lid closed with a bang! Their struggles set the trunk in motion. It began to roll on its wheels, from the wall to the door, which stood ajar. As there was no threshold to the door, the trunk rolled out into the yard, and from there into the street. The struggle inside sent it moving down the narrow thoroughfare. The street sloped towards the Synagogue, whose door was wide open. With a clatter the trunk rolled right into the Synagogue!

A near panic broke out among the worshippers. Their shrieks and screams were heard by the women and children, who came running to see what was happening in the house of worship.

Strange voices were heard inside the trunk. Helm became frightened . . . surely the trunk was full of demons! The congregation stood petrified, and the Rabbi was about to begin reciting Psalms, a sure weapon against demons. But the trunk stopped suddenly, jammed between two benches.

Berel the Beadle approached it carefully. Quietly reciting the proper verses for protection against demons, he raised the lid and . . . Yossel-Zissel and Sossie were lying

there, exhausted . . . he bareheaded, and she without a wig! "Woe to the eyes that behold such a sight!" cried the Rabbi.

He turned to the congregation.

"Right after the holiday, a Town Meeting must be called!"

It was one of the stormiest meetings in the history of Helm. There were extremists who demanded that Yossel-Zissel should not be permitted to teach. He wasn't fit to instruct children! The Rabbi of Helm brushed this aside with a wave of the hand.

"You don't deprive a man of his livelihood, even for wanton wickedness, because depriving a man of his livelihood means in truth a death sentence; and not only for him, but also for his family."

Others insisted Yossel-Zissel be fined heavily, say, five rubles. But the Rabbi objected again.

"If you fine a rich man you punish him—him alone. But if you fine a poor man, you also punish his children. You deprive them of food. These little lambs, what have they done?"

So, after much argument and discussion, Helm enacted the following ordinance, to prevent the recurrence of such a disgrace:

> a. No trunk should have wheels. This applies to all the trunks in Helm now. Their wheels must be removed immediately.

b. Every door in Helm must be provided, as of now, this day, with a high threshold.

c. No *melamed* can live on Synagogue Street. This does not apply to Yossel-Zissel, because a law can't be retroactive. Besides, it would impose a hardship on his family.

The extremists pressed for a fourth ordinance: "No *melamed* should covet blintzes." But again, the Rabbi and the more sober citizens objected. This would sound like adding an eleventh commandment to the Ten Commandments. The Tenth Commandment reads: "Thou shall not covet your neighbor's wife, his man-servant, his woman-servant, his ox, his mule and all that belongs to your neighbor." First, there is not a word mentioned about blintzes. Second, Yossel-Zissel does not covet somebody else's blintzes. He wants his own. That's not a sin.

They wrote the three ordinances into the Town Record. Thenceforth, all Helm observed them.

The enchanted goat

TEN YEARS PASSED. THE TOWN FORGOT ABOUT
the trunk and the blintzes—but not Yossel-Zissel! True,
he never spoke again of his craving for blintzes, not even
to Sossie. But he always thought about them . . . yellow
as saffron, the dough kneaded with pure yolks of fresh
eggs, the cheese rich with butter, all three layers drenched
with cream! He thought about them during the day,
dreamed about them at night.

Ten years! The children were growing up. The eldest
son and the older daughter had married. The other
children were less dependent on their parents, and Yossel-
Zissel began to save money secretly. Even Sossie didn't
know about it.

One fine morning, in the month of Elul, at the end of
the school year, he broke the news to Sossie. "I've saved
up twelve rubles—a ten ruble gold piece and two silver
cart-wheels. Now, we can buy a goat."

Sossie was ready to give her husband a piece of her
mind: She had been skimping and saving, working her
fingers to the bone to prepare a Sabbath befitting a Jewish

home. Last year she had borrowed money to make a dress for Hinde, their fourth child, who had outgrown her dress. And all the time, her dear husband sat on twelve rubles cash and kept quiet, as if he were made of stone!

But she was so overwhelmed by the news that she cried out joyfully, against her will, "A goat! Now, we'll begin to live!"

Husband and wife sat down to talk over their good fortune. They decided to inquire carefully where to buy the goat.

All Helm was of one mind. The best place to buy a goat is in Goatsville, a village four miles from Helm. The best goat raiser is Fishke the Lame. He drives a hard bargain, but he's honest.

Before Yossel-Zissel departed for Goatsville, Sossie warned, "I know that Fishke is honest, but keep your eyes open! Twelve rubles is a hoard of money. You should get a goat which gives at least a quart of milk at a time. Don't trust Fishke too much. The only One that can be trusted in money matters is the Almighty, because everything belongs to Him. But people! Oh, they're greedy and grasping!"

Yossel-Zissel made a wry face; he never liked slander. But he wouldn't argue now, not with twelve live rubles in his pocket, and a milk goat waiting for him. So he muttered assent as a dutiful husband does, "I'll watch myself. They won't fool me," and left for Goatsville.

Everything would have been fine, and Yossel-Zissel surely would have brought back a milk goat . . . if not for that imp, Moishke.

82 Moishke was the son of Michael, keeper of an inn which stood halfway between Helm and Goatsville. Since Michael was the only Jew in the little hamlet, he had sent his son to school in Helm. Moishke was a spoiled and stubborn boy, big for his age and hard to handle. Michael charged Yossel-Zissel not to spare the rod, but to discipline the unruly lad.

Moishke did not submit easily to discipline, and Yossel-Zissel was an old hand in handling unruly children. So, as the saying goes, "A scythe hit a stone and sparks flew."

The boy developed a special hatred for the teacher, not just because of punishments meted out to him, but because Yossel-Zissel never became angry. He was always calm, collected and methodical. Moreover, when he punished Moishke he chanted a ditty of his own composition:

> One and one are two,
> Two and two are four.
> Don't struggle and don't wiggle
> Or I'll give you more.

Yossel-Zissel did it methodically: "One [whack] and one [another whack] are two [two whacks]. Two [whacks] and two [whacks] are four [four really smart blows]. Don't struggle [if the child struggled, a real blow], don't

wiggle [a pause and then, bang!]. Or . . . [pause] I'll give you more [sharp, stinging blows, one after another]."

For two years the teacher and the boy were at war. Then Moishke became Bar Mitzvah and his schooling ended. But he didn't forget Yossel-Zissel. He'd get revenge some day!

That day came on the Sunday morning Yossel-Zissel went to Goatsville. On the first mile, the *melamed's* heart was light and his step brisk. It was cool, and walking was pleasant. But, as the sun rose, Yossel-Zissel began to perspire and chafe. He was glad when he saw the inn ahead.

When Yossel-Zissel stepped into the inn, Michael received him joyfully. "Oh, what an honor, Rebbe! Where are you going so early in the morning?"

"I'm going to Goatsville to buy a goat. Praised be the Lord, I have twelve rubles cash in my pocket. For that sum I can have my pick. But now, I'm tired and thirsty. Get me a cold drink. A cool glass of *kvass* will be just right. It will refresh me."

The innkeeper called out, "Moishke, get the Rebbe some cold *kvass* from the cellar, and an egg bagel. Step lively, don't let the Rebbe wait!"

When Moishke brought the refreshments, Yossel-Zissel looked at him in amazement. "Why, the boy's only fifteen, and is already tall as a sapling and has the neck of a bull!" He giggled, "Well, Moishke, I don't think that

I could put you over my knee and begin to sing my 'one and one are two' with a birch rod in my right hand."

"You want to try it with both hands, Rebbe?" Moishke asked, wryly.

His father flew into a rage.

"What kind of talk is that to a Rebbe? Is that respect for a teacher! Apologize or I'll skin you alive!" Michael stood a head taller and a hundred pounds heavier than his son, so he could enforce his command. Moishke reddened and muttered an apology.

In Goatsville, Yossel-Zissel went directly to Fishke the Lame. He did not mince words.

"Listen, Fishke, you're a pious, God-fearing and honest Jew. I came here to buy a goat. I want a good goat. She must give at least two quarts of milk a day. Now, do you have a goat like that? If you do, well and good; otherwise, tell me where I can get one."

Fishke looked at him. "There's only one place you can get a good goat—from Fishke the Lame. How much money do you have?"

"Twelve rubles, Fishke."

"Well, for twelve rubles I'll sell you a goat which gives four quarts of milk a day! No, eleven will be enough. I'm an honest trader."

"Well and good!" said Yossel-Zissel, joyfully. "I trust you, but still I want to see it with my own eyes."

"Fine, fine! Here's a bucket." Fishke called his wife, Zlate. A dark woman, sunburned and sturdy, entered.

"You may go with her to the stall to watch her milk the goat," he told the *melamed*.

"It isn't proper," Yossel-Zissel stammered, reddening. "I trust her. She can milk the goat alone and bring the milk here."

Zlate silently left the room. After a while she returned with half a bucket of foaming warm milk. Yossel-Zissel measured it. There were more than two quarts in the bucket!

When he had paid the eleven rubles, Zlate pointed out his goat. "It's the black nanny goat with the white patch on her forehead, in the second stall."

"Believe me, it's the best goat in the flock!" said Fishke. "But it's getting late. Stay over night, and tomorrow, right after morning prayers, you'll leave for Helm. Then you'll have a chance to measure the goat's milk a second time. And we'll also be honored to have you as our guest for the night."

Yossel-Zissel agreed. The next morning the goat yielded even more. Fishke tied a rope around its neck and handed the other end to Yossel-Zissel. A slap on the goat's flank, and the Helmite and his prize were on their way home.

It was hard going. The day was hot and the road was dusty. The goat liked to stop and nip the grass beside the

road, and often had to be dragged. Yossel-Zissel arrived at the inn, wilted. Michael immediately told Moishke to take care of the goat. Yossel-Zissel sat at a table, mopping his brow, while Michael served him a nice meal and a cool drink of *kvass*. As Yossel-Zissel ate and drank with relish, he told Michael about his purchase and praised Fishke's honesty.

While Yossel-Zissel sat in the inn, Moishke fed and watered the goat, thinking, "That cold-blooded Cossack, that murderer—he bought a fine goat. Too bad . . . Fishke the Lame is as honest as a Rabbi."

Then he noticed the white patch on the goat's forehead. "Why that nanny goat looks just like our billy goat!" A light came into his eye. "Here's where I get even!"

He tied the billy goat to the post and hurried the nanny goat into the stall. When the switch was completed, he sauntered into the inn, whistling.

"I didn't know Reb Yossel-Zissel was an expert on goats," he told Michael. "I'm telling you, Father, he got a bargain! The goat's worth fourteen rubles."

Yossel-Zissel laughed happily. "A man who knows our Holy Torah is smart enough to be a connoisseur on everything, even on goats."

Moishke nodded. "I see you're right. Yes, sir!"

Michael slapped his son lovingly on his back.

"Now, you'll have respect for your Rebbe. You see that Torah makes men wise."

"You're right, Father. I'm young, but I'm willing to learn," answered Moishke with a gleam in his eye.

Yossel-Zissel rose from the table, happy and content. "I see that the paddlings I gave you worked. You grew up a fine lad. I trust you'll never forget what I did for you."

"Oh, no, Rebbe, I haven't forgotten, and I never will forget!"

Yossel-Zissel went out to the stall. He saw the remains of the fodder in the trough and noted the round sides of the goat.

"A fine boy—he fed the animal as if it were his own!"

He patted the goat, untied it, and started for Helm.

He arrived home at dusk, and entered the house, shouting, "Sossie, get a bucket and a stool!"

Sossie looked at him and shrugged.

"Look at his excitement! I already prepared a bucket and a stool. Did you bring a goat?"

"Did I bring a goat? Wait till you see it! It's a bargain at fourteen rubles, but I paid only eleven. It gives four quarts of milk a day!"

Sossie waved disparagingly. "I'll be satisfied with three."

"Four quarts, I tell you—not a drop less! Now, hurry! It's past milking time. For supper I want groats with milk."

As Sossie left, bucket in hand, Yossel-Zissel stood up to say his evening prayers. He had scarcely begun the first Psalm when Sossie rushed into the house and slammed the bucket down.

"He bought a goat! It's a nanny goat like I'm a lantern! When a fool goes to market, all the storekeepers rejoice. 'Go milk it,' he says! How can I milk a billy goat?"

Yossel-Zissel forgot that he was in the middle of his prayers and mustn't interrupt them. He exclaimed:

"A *what*?"

"A billy goat, I say, and it has eyes as stupid as yours."

"But I saw the milk she gave! I saw it myself with my own eyes!"

"Of course, you saw milk, my scholarly husband! But did you see where the milk came from?"

Yossel-Zissel scratched his head.

"Well, it's true I didn't see her milk the goat, but I can hardly believe that a pious, upright Jew like Fishke would cheat. . . . But if you say it's a billy goat . . . well, I suppose you know. . . . But don't worry! Tomorrow I'll return this he-goat to Fishke and what a tongue-lashing he'll get from me!"

Right after dawn, Yossel-Zissel and the billy goat set out toward Goatsville. He was in a hurry and had not intended to stop at the inn, but his desire to talk about his troubles overwhelmed him. Michael was astonished to see him walk in again.

"What are you doing here again, Rebbe?"

"All the plagues of Pharaoh on our enemies' heads! Fishke fooled me! He sold me a nanny goat and then substituted a billy goat. He thinks I'll be quiet about it, but I'm going to take him to the Rabbi for an account. He'll be fined as sure as it's Tuesday now in God's world."

Moishke, busy at the other end of the room, called out, "Rebbe, the poor animal must be thirsty. I'll give it water."

"You're right," answered Yossel-Zissel. "May God reward you for your good heart."

Moishke hurried to the stall, replaced the billy goat with the nanny goat, and returned to the inn.

Yossel-Zissel did not tarry. He hurried on to Goatsville, seething with righteous anger.

He entered Fishke's house, scolding. "Cheat, swindler, thief! I came to you because I depended upon your honesty! I paid you what you asked without bargaining or haggling, but you cheated me. No, you didn't cheat me, you robbed me—substituting a he-goat for a she-goat is just robbery!"

Fishke stood in the middle of the room, eyes bulging, looking as if someone were speaking to him in a foreign language. Finally, he found words.

"Didn't I give you the nanny goat with the white patch on her forehead?"

"The goat has a white patch on its forehead, but it's a nanny goat like a chimney sweep is a scullery maid, like two times two is chicken soup. It's a nanny goat like a bull is a milk cow."

Fishke interrupted, impatiently.

"Will you close the faucet of your samovar for a while? Where's the nanny goat?"

"Your nanny goat," answered Yossel-Zissel sarcastically, "is standing in the yard, tied to the gate post."

"Let me look at it."

Out in the yard, Fishke shot a glance at the goat, and turned to Yossel-Zissel. "The sun must have made a *kashe* out of your brains! Here stands my best goat, her udder overfull because you didn't milk her, you idiot, and you tell me she's a billy goat! Stay here, you brainless Helmite, and watch her. I'll bring a bucket and milk her right in front of your eyes."

Any other time, Yossel-Zissel would have started a fight with anyone who called him "a brainless Helmite," but he was so taken aback at Fishke's offer to milk the billy goat that he stood, open-mouthed.

Fishke brought a stool and a bucket, sat down, patted the goat on the flanks and began to milk. The goat bleated with relief, and Yossel-Zissel stood, eyes popping.

Fishke thrust the bucket at him.

"Look, smarty! It's not well water and it's not rain water. It's a bucket full of warm, foaming goat milk."

He slammed the bucket down. "The goat is yours, the milk is yours, and get out of my sight!" With that, Fishke stalked into the house.

Yossel-Zissel dipped his finger into the milk and dabbed it on his tongue. Yes, it tasted like milk. He raised the bucket to his nose. Yes, it smelled like milk. He stood, deep in thought. What should he do with the bucket of milk? At length he set it on Fishke's porch, with a sigh untied the goat, and left for Helm.

Yossel-Zissel was morose and angry with himself. He had accused an honest, pious Jew of dishonesty. He should have been firmer with Sossie and insisted that the animal was a nanny goat, not a billy goat. He had taken her word for it, made a fool of himself and insulted an upright and just man.

When the *melamed* reached the inn, Michael was not there. Moishke, happy and carefree, called out, "Well, Rebbe, how did you make out?"

"I made a fool of myself," answered Yossel-Zissel. "It's a nanny goat. I'm so exhausted, I don't have the strength to bring it to the stall. Take it and give it water while I rest up. Just serve me a glass of *kvass*. I'm not hungry."

Moishke took the goat and exchanged it for the billy goat with the same markings. He served a tall glass of

cold *kvass* to Yossel-Zissel. The Rebbe did not tarry. He took the billy goat and left.

By the time he reached Helm, his spirits had risen. He had been right in the first place—it was a fine milk goat. Sossie didn't know what she was talking about. Hadn't he seen Fishke milk her?

He walked into the house before dusk, calling, "Sossie, take the bucket and attend to the goat! Now, you can't tell me that I was fooled! Fishke milked the goat while I was looking. I saw the bucket of foaming warm milk." He repeated Fishke's witticism, "and it wasn't well water or rain water—it was goat's milk."

Sossie did not answer. Silently, she took the bucket and went out in the yard. Immediately she was back.

"So he milked it right in front of your eyes," she hissed. "Then you are blind! It's a billy goat!"

Yossel-Zissel began to shout. "Don't tell me it's a billy goat! You're deaf, dumb and blind! It even bleats like a nanny goat. I say it is a nanny goat!"

"And how does a nanny goat bleat, tell me? *I* am deaf, dumb and blind? You're a fool and a dullard! Even in Shedlitz you would be a simpleton!"

Neighbors began to gather. Many of the women examined the goat. No question about it—it was a male goat.

When Yossel-Zissel heard this, he sighed. There was only one thing to do.

"Tomorrow I'll go to the Rabbi and have him certify

that it's a billy goat. Then I'll take the billy goat and the certificate to the Rabbi of Goatsville and call Fishke to account. There's still law and order around here, and a man can't cheat his fellowman and get away with it."

The next day Yossel-Zissel and Sossie brought the goat to the Rabbi of Helm. The Rabbi heard their story and called in two women who owned goats to examine Yossel-Zissel's goat. They testified that it was, indeed, a billy goat. Then the Rabbi wrote a letter to the Rabbi of Goatsville, concluding, "Whereas Fishke sold Yossel-Zissel a nanny goat which upon the testimony of two expert witnesses was found to be a billy goat, this is a clear case of cheating. Therefore, the Rabbi of Goatsville should see to it that justice is done; namely, that Yossel-Zissel either gets his money back from Fishke or any nanny goat of his choosing. Also, as is customary among Jews, the culprit should be fined in the form of a contribution to charity."

Yossel-Zissel took the letter and the billy goat, and left for Goatsville a third time, still vexed and angry, but feeling that justice was on his side and that the matter would at last be settled.

When he approached the inn, Yossel-Zissel remembered that in all the turmoil he had forgotten to eat breakfast or to feed the animal. Michael was still away, but Moishke came running, his voice raised in feigned surprise.

94

"What happened, Rebbe? You're back again!"

Yossel-Zissel sighed.

"Moishke, I don't know how Fishke managed to switch goats. With my own eyes I saw him milking it. I never lost sight of it. Still, when I brought the nanny goat to Helm it turned out that Fishke, may his name be obliterated from the congregation of Israel, gave me a billy goat in place of the nanny goat."

Moishke clucked his tongue. "A scoundrel and a rogue!"

"But I got him this time," said Yossel-Zissel with assurance. "Right in my pocket there's a letter from the Rabbi of Helm to the Rabbi of Goatsville. The Rabbi will fine Fishke a nice sum for charity and I'll pick out the best nanny goat for my money."

"I'm glad it will finally be settled," Moishke observed, piously.

"In the meantime, Moishke, attend to the animal, and then give me a bite. I haven't had breakfast yet."

Moishke hurried to the stall. He replaced the nanny goat and returned to the inn. As he served a hearty breakfast to Yossel-Zissel, he laughed to himself, "He'll need his strength when he gets to Goatsville!"

Yossel-Zissel went straight to the house of the Goatsville Rabbi, and told him his story. The Rabbi of Goatsville read the letter from the Rabbi of Helm and sighed to himself. "Of course, 'A man will transgress for a piece of

bread,' but Fishke is not poor." He stopped himself, horrified. "Why, I condemned the man without a hearing!" He looked up and called to the beadle, "Summon Fishke and his wife!"

Fishke arrived in a black mood. Before the Rabbi had a chance to ask a question, he burst out, "Rabbi, I see the nuisance is here again. Honestly, I don't know what this Helmite wants! I sold him my best goat—the black one with the white patch on its forehead. It gives four quarts of milk a day! He offered me twelve rubles and I told him eleven was enough. But two days ago he came back . . ."

The Rabbi interrupted him. "Fishke, calm down. You don't even know what . . ."

"I can guess, Rabbi! He'll accuse me of selling him a he-goat, the way he did two days ago. But, . . ."

"Quiet, Fishke! I have a paper from the Rabbi of Helm certifying that it was a billy goat Yossel-Zissel brought from Goatsville."

"I don't know what the Rabbi of Helm saw. All I know is that I sold this Helmite a fine she-goat which gives four quarts of milk a day. Wait, Rabbi!" Fishke turned to Yossel-Zissel. "Did you bring the nanny goat I sold you with the white patch on its forehead?"

"Of course," Yossel-Zissel answered. "It has a white patch on its forehead, but it's a billy goat."

Fishke turned to the Rabbi. "Come, Rabbi, take a look at it. My Zlate will milk it."

"Let the Rebbetzin come, too," answered the Rabbi. "And my two associates, as witnesses."

They all went into the yard. The goat, tied to the post, bleated pitifully. Zlate, Fishke's wife, struck her hand on her thighs.

"Poor beast, it's uncomfortable. They haven't milked her since yesterday!"

Zlate didn't lose a moment. She sat down and milked the goat. Before long the bucket was almost full.

Yossel-Zissel stood there, shocked and confused. He stammered, "I don't know. Surely this is a nanny goat; but in Helm it was a billy goat!"

Fishke gave him a withering look.

"Rabbi, I don't want to be bothered with him any more. Please write a paper testifying that this is a nanny goat and not a billy goat. Let him take it back to Helm and let me be! He is the guilty one! He ought to be fined for accusing me falsely."

"Tut, tut!" said the Rabbi. "If we fine Yossel-Zissel, we make a liar of the Rabbi of Helm. He certified that the goat was a billy goat in Helm. We weren't there, so we don't know what happened. We can only certify that the goat Yossel-Zissel brought here was a nanny goat. And this we shall do."

The Rabbi of Goatsville wrote the Rabbi of Helm that the goat which Yossel-Zissel brought to Goatsville had been examined and found to be a nanny goat.

The certificate was written on parchment, as are all important documents. It was stamped with the Rabbi's seal and signed by the two witnesses. When all was completed, Yossel-Zissel had one more request.

"Please, Rabbi, make another copy of it on the back of the certificate, in case I lose one."

The Rabbi of Goatsville fulfilled his request and wrote the same text on the other side of the parchment.

Yossel-Zissel started home with the goat. His head was light and his heart was joyous. Now Sossie couldn't call him simpleton, dullard, fool, and what not! In his pocket was a certificate written on both sides, two copies, in case one got lost; a certificate signed by the Rabbi and two witnesses, and stamped with the congregational seal, attesting to the fact that the goat he had bought from Fishke was a nanny goat.

He stopped at the inn to celebrate his good fortune. The innkeeper had returned from his business trip and Yossel-Zissel told him the whole story. Curious, Michael went to the stall to look at the animal. He came back and told Yossel-Zissel, "Really, it's a fine nanny goat. Fishke certainly didn't cheat you. This calls for a drink!" He turned to Moishke. "I'll serve the Rebbe. You go and water the goat."

Well, Yossel-Zissel had his drink, and Moishke—you know what he did.

"Sossie," Yossel-Zissel shouted at the door, "go and milk the goat! For supper I want rice soup with pure milk. And don't talk back to me . . . it's a nanny goat! Thursday I want blintzes. Real blintzes, like . . ."

Sossie didn't answer. She stalked out to the stall. She was back immediately, slamming the bucket and the stool on the floor.

"So you want blintzes on Thursday? You can have stones fried in nettles, or fritters made of yellow clay—take your choice! Tell me, what kind of an idiot are you to be fooled three times? You brought a billy goat again!"

Yossel-Zissel stood, petrified. Then he stammered, in a whisper, "It—it can't be."

"What do you mean, it can't be? It *is*! Am I blind? It's a billy goat! Nothing but a billy goat!"

"It can't be! I have a certificate from the Rabbi of Goatsville, signed by two witnesses and stamped with the congregational seal, that says it's a nanny goat."

Sossie's voice rose to a screech.

"I don't care if it's certified by a special assembly of a hundred Rabbis. It's still a billy goat! And you, idiot, where were *your* eyes?"

Yossel-Zissel found his tongue.

"Silence, woman!" he thundered. "It's not so simple! There's a deep mystery here. Of course, I used my eyes. Eight pairs of eyes saw that it was a nanny goat, and yet it turned out to be a billy goat for the third time. Keep

quiet! After the evening prayer I'll take the goat and the certificate to our Rabbi. Let *him* solve the mystery."

100 Quite a crowd gathered in Yossel-Zissel's yard. All agreed that Yossel-Zissel was right. It wasn't as simple as Sossie thought.

Well, Yossel-Zissel brought the goat and the certificate to the Rabbi. Again the Rebbetzin examined the goat. "Yes," she said, "it's a billy goat."

The Rabbi studied the certificate—the Rabbi of Goatsville and his two associates had certified that this was a nanny goat! No, it was too deep a mystery even for him. He called a Town Meeting.

The best heads of Helm sat seven days and seven nights, sifting the evidence, and could arrive at no solution. On the eighth day, Gimpel the Mayor jumped up. "I have it! It's so simple that we overlooked it!"

The Rabbi took a good snuff of tobacco and gave a hearty sneeze. "What's so simple that we overlooked it?"

"Rabbi, years ago the watermill was built on top of the mountain, according to plans drawn up by our best architects. Still, it didn't work. We tried everything, but the watermill on top of the mountain didn't turn. Finally, a Town Meeting decided that the climate of Helm wasn't suitable for watermills. It's the same with the goat. When a nanny goat is brought to Helm, it turns into a billy goat because of the climate."

Two resolutions were adopted:

1. Resolved: Yossel-Zissel is not a dullard as his wife Sossie claims. He's not an idiot who can be fooled. Neither is Fishke a cheat. He did sell a nanny goat to Yossel-Zissel. But when Yossel-Zissel brought the nanny goat into Helm, the climate changed it into a billy goat.

2. It is also resolved that the event be written in the Town Record, followed by the above resolution, all in capital letters, so that it can't be missed.

As a matter of fact, the story has a happy ending. About a week later, Michael noticed that his billy goat was missing and that he had an extra nanny goat in his stall—a nanny goat that was as much like Yossel-Zissel's billy goat as one drop of water is to another. Michael knew his son Moishke, and understood what had happened. But he also knew that if he told the true story no one in Helm would believe him. When something is recorded in the Town Record, it becomes fact—the undeniable, irrefutable truth. So, one dark night he came to Helm and exchanged the goats.

In the morning Sossie discovered that the billy goat had turned into a nanny goat! She assumed that this was due to the change in weather—autumn had begun. The whole town agreed with her.

Beinush, the alert policeman

AFTER THE RAILROAD CAME TO HELM, THERE was a great influx of strangers in town. The newcomers did not obey the laws of the city, and many reforms had to be instituted.

Helm already had a Town Prison. It consisted of a wooden fence with two small holes in it. When a culprit was punished, he had to put his arms through the two holes. Then two barrel hoops were placed in his hands. A guard wasn't needed, because nobody was strong enough to pull the big iron hoops through the holes!

But when the strangers began to come, the unheard-of happened. Prisoners dropped the hoops without permission, pulled their hands out of the holes, and walked quietly away!

To make matters worse, as the population increased, the offenders grew in number. There were often four or five inmates at a time, but there was only one fence with two holes—a prison for one.

Then the town built a real prison with cells which

were kept under lock and key. They also organized a police force.

The police force consisted of officers and plain-clothes men. The entire force was active by day, when there were crowds in the streets and the stores were open. It kept order and had an eye out for shoplifters and thieves.

At night, when the stores were closed and the houses were locked, only one policeman was on duty. One— but a good one!

Beinush was a burly fellow, as brave as he was strong. People said he could see at night because he had one cat's eye and one owl's eye.

He was fearless. He even dared to wear a sheepskin coat, fur side out, big city style. He wasn't afraid a wolf might mistake him for a sheep. "Let him attack!" he would say. "I'll split his head with my cudgel."

The police chief knew that the town could depend on Beinush, who not only was an excellent policeman, but also a true Helmite; a descendant of one of the early settlers of Helm.

The thieves heard of Beinush's prowess and kept away from Helm. They went to other towns where there was easier picking.

But one dark, rainy night, Beinush saw someone trying to break into a store. He collared the thief.

"A plague on you, rascal! You thought that on a cold rainy night like this, Beinush would tuck himself somewhere in a warm corner! I've a notion to give your neck one little twist, so you'll do your thieving someplace above the clouds! But the law says I have to bring you to the station house without rumpling your hair, and I uphold the law. Come on! Off to jail! I'll let the judge take care of you."

The prisoner began to whine.

"Please, have a heart! I know you talk rough, but you're a good guy. Give me a break, and let me go! I

swear I'll never leave my house after dark. Look at the size of me! Do I look like a thief—a skinny runt like me?"

But Beinush was tough.

"I know better than to trust a crook," he jeered. "I wish you'd resist. Just a little—so I could flatten you! You may be little and skinny, but you're a big thief. . . ."

Beinush stopped, as a suspicious thought popped into his mind. "He's puny, all right—not much of a thief or a man. Maybe he's a decoy sent by the real thieves! Didn't he make a bit too much noise, as if he wanted to be caught? If I take him to the station house, the town will be left unguarded, and the real thieves will go to work!"

He stood, deep in thought, clutching the runt. "What'll I do now?"

Then a brilliant idea came to mind. When he had misbehaved in *cheder* as a child, the Rebbe had put him in a corner with a broom upside down in his hands. He couldn't leave until the Rebbe gave him permission!

Beinush fixed an eye on the thief. "I can't take you to the police station and leave the city unguarded. Here, I'm putting you in this corner, to stay till morning. At daybreak I'll pick you up and bring you to the station. Just remember, you can't leave!"

Yes, Beinush put a stick in the thief's hand. He knew a broom would have been better, but he was in too much of a hurry to look for one. "A stick will do in an emergency," he thought.

Beinush left the prisoner standing between two houses and went on to patrol the city. At dawn he returned, but to his surprise, there wasn't a trace of the thief or of the stick. How had the crook dared leave without permission? He must have been an out-of-towner! No Helmite would be so unprincipled.

Beinush reported at the police station. "I caught a thief, but he was so puny, I immediately realized that he was only a decoy to make me leave my post, so that the real thieves could have a clear field. So I put him in a corner, with instructions not to leave till dawn. But he disobeyed orders and escaped."

The chief of police listened attentively.

"Beinush, you did a fine job, catching the thief and avoiding his trap. Go to sleep so you can be rested for your night duty."

Beinush slept a whole day and awoke before sunset. He took a length of rope with him when he went on duty, besides his club.

Just after midnight, his sharp eyes spied the same thief trying to break a lock. With a leap, Beinush pounced on him.

"Aha, I got you again! I've a mind to smack my club over your legs just once, and fix you so you won't run any more! But the law says I mustn't even muss your tie, and I'm an officer of the law, sworn to uphold it. So, step lively!"

Then Beinush remembered! "But this little speck of a man can't be the real danger! It's obvious: If I leave my post, the real thieves will have a heyday."

He smiled, shrewdly.

"All right, so you escaped last night! You fooled me. But Beinush can be fooled only once. I brought some rope

along and I'll take care of you the way my mother took care of a wandering chicken. She tied one end of the rope to the hen's leg and the other end to the bedpost. We don't have a bedpost here, but we have doorknobs. I know what to do."

Beinush tied the thief's leg to the doorknob. "I'll pick you up in the morning."

Well, at dawn he came back and the prisoner was gone! Beinush was more surprised than the night before. Had the chicken tied to the bedpost ever escaped?

Beinush reported smartly: "I caught the thief again and made extra sure he wouldn't escape. I tied his leg to a doorknob, the way you tie up a chicken. But he got away. He certainly knew I wanted him to stay there until dawn, but he went anyhow. He's no good!"

The officer in charge was equally astonished. He commended Beinush for his quick-wittedness, as well as for catching the thief two nights straight. The prisoner was plain irresponsible! The officer told Beinush not to worry. After all, the offender was an outsider. A Helmite would never be so unmannerly or unreliable.

Beinush went home and slept well. He awoke before sunset, refreshed and alert, and reported for duty that night.

At midnight he came across the same fellow, climbing into a store. Down came Beinush's big paw on the crook's neck, as he shouted with glee, "So, you got away twice! I

wish I could slap you around a little to teach you manners! But I'm an officer of the law and I'm supposed to bring you back in one piece. But don't get any ideas this time. I'm wise to all your tricks! I won't put you in a corner because you'd escape without leave. I won't tie your foot to a door because you'd untie the knot. Even a chicken is more honest than you are! Tonight you'll stay with me till dawn. You'll walk my beat with me. You'll march till your feet feel like hot coals.

"At dawn, after I finished my tour, I'll take you in and turn you over to the judge. Then there'll be reckoning! I won't spare you! I'll report to him everything you did! I'll tell him that not only did you try to ransack the stores of Helm three times, but you were so unmannerly that after you were caught, you used some trick each time and escaped. Yes, you escaped justice!"

All night long Beinush walked his beat, in his right hand a club and his left hand on the thief's collar. When dawn broke, he turned back to the police station. As they approached the station house, a wind tore the thief's hat from his head. The prisoner began to plead.

"Please, officer, let me catch my hat! It's brand new! Honest, I'll come right back!"

"You think you can fool me a third time?" Beinush jeered. "If I let you go after the hat, you'll return like yesterday will return. You stay *right here* and *I'll* run after the hat!"

Beinush reported to his superior officer: "I watched him all night long. I made him walk my beat with me. But when I left him alone for one moment, while I went after his hat, he escaped. The sneak knew very well that he was supposed to stand there until I came back."

The officer was amazed.

"Beinush, you're the best policeman on the force! You caught the thief three nights straight! It's not your fault he got away. You were logical, but the thief wasn't. What can you expect from an outsider? Your valor and diligence will be reported and you'll be rewarded."

Beinush *was* rewarded. The commissioner decided that a resourceful, courageous policeman like Beinush was too good to walk a beat. He was promoted to captain.

The River Shore Club

III

THE RIVER SHORE CLUB IS THE OLDEST AND MOST exclusive club in Helm. Originally it had not been founded as an exclusive social club. It came into existence after a calamity in which three people drowned.

Helm, at that time, was a village on the banks of the river. There was an old superstition among the people that every spring, when the ice melted, someone must drown. It was believed that the river spirit demanded a sacrifice: It was angry because it had been locked up all winter under the thick ice.

That spring a child was swept away in the torrents when the ice broke. The Helmites took this as an unavoidable calamity. The parents mourned, the people sympathized with them, and that was that.

But in midsummer three important burghers went for a swim and all three of them drowned. This was another matter! Something had to be done about it!

Immediately, a Town Meeting was called to find a way to prevent another such calamity. An ordinance was passed, forbidding swimming in the river except in groups of ten, with a leader to supervise.

Eventually, the ordinance went unobserved except by descendants of the original settlers, who formed a society that swam in tens. In the beginning everyone who took it upon himself to observe the ancient ordinance could become a member of the group. But as time passed, the club emblem came to be a mark of distinction and only blue-blooded Helmites were accepted as members.

No one remembers how it came about that the club members began to wear a distinct uniform when they went swimming. The uniform consisted of a red shirt and pants trimmed with blue tape. The shirt had a stiff collar with two embroidered blue fish and two rows of gold buttons down the front. A flat cap with a tassel and a blue plaited belt completed the uniform.

Each group of ten was headed by a leader. The swimmers marched two abreast, military fashion, the leader at their head. On the leader's sleeve was a beautifully embroidered whip.

Why a whip? There was a reason for it, and, of course, a story.

Years and years back, Todros, the great, great grandson of Eliokin Getzl, the first mayor of Helm, became president of the River Shore Club.

One hot summer afternoon he took a group of twenty

for a swim. Because he was president, he was not content to march at the head of ten. He led a group of twenty.

He was a great disciplinarian, unduly mindful of the smallest detail. He arranged his group two abreast, according to height. The shirts with the standing collars were buttoned carefully, the belts pulled tight around the waist, and the buttons brightly polished. Todros instructed the group to follow him, not only in step, but also in every other detail.

And they did. They marched with his exact gait. When he took out his handkerchief and wiped his perspiring forehead, they did the same. When he coughed, twenty men echoed his cough. When he blew his nose, the twenty did likewise.

When they came to the river, they did not undress in a haphazard way. They followed his lead and imitated him exactly.

He left a man on the shore to keep an eye on the bathers. He was a strict follower of rules and did not overlook anything.

After they came out of the water, the swimmers stretched out on the beach and told the guard to go for a swim. When they all had had their sun bath and had dressed, they were ready to fall in line to march home. But Todros sprang to his feet and addressed them in the flowery language he loved.

"Men, do not rush! Caution is the father of wisdom.

Haste leads to error, and error leads to calamity. Besides, he who runs too fast, stumbles and falls. What I mean is: Twenty-one of us came to the beach. Shouldn't twenty-one return?"

"Of course!"

"Then we must take a count. How do we know that no one drowned?"

"Woe to us," they began to wail. "We're all married men—fathers of children and husbands of wives. Whoever drowned left a widow and orphans. Who will feed them? Who will clothe them and who will take care of their schooling?"

"Quiet!" commanded Todros, angrily. "We don't know yet whom to bewail. Wait till we find out who drowned! Stand in line and I'll count you."

They all stood in formation as he counted, Helmite-fashion, to avert the "evil eye."

"Not one, not two, not three, not four, not five . . . not twenty," he finished.

"Not more than twenty, Todros? But we were twenty-one," said one of the bathers.

Pale and trembling, Todros answered, "Only twenty."

They opened their mouths to burst out in a wail, but Todros stopped them with a motion of his hand.

"There's nothing to be alarmed about yet. First we must check if I counted right. Let me figure out how to check this in a more reliable manner."

They all waited silently, while Todros wrinkled his forehead, deep in thought. Finally, his face brightened.

"I have it! Before, I counted you from right to left. Now, I'll count you from left to right."

He counted again. "Not one, not two, not three . . . not twenty. No more!"

Todros repeated silently, "Twenty and no more! My first count was right."

Out loud he called, "Brethren of the Shore Club of Helm, we have lost a man!"

A shrill wail pierced the quiet of the summer afternoon. Todros stood helpless. He had no words to comfort them.

A rider who passed heard the lament. He turned his horse to the bank of the river and stopped at the group.

"Burghers of Helm, why are you crying? What has happened?"

"A great calamity has befallen us! Twenty-one of us went swimming, but only twenty came out of the water," answered Todros.

The rider looked over the group and counted the bathers with a glance.

"Did you count them?"

"Of course, I did," answered Todros. "Here, see for yourself." He gave a command: "Stand in a straight line and be counted!" He counted the men again.

The horseman laughed. "Clever Helmite, you forgot to count yourself!"

Todros' face beamed.

"You're right! I did forget to count myself. Thank you for bringing it to my attention. Now I'll count again—and will include myself also."

He gave a sharp command: "Men, fall in!"

The horseman turned toward the river to water his horse.

While the horse was drinking, Todros counted. He was careful not to forget himself. He started to count from himself: "Not one, not two . . . twenty-two!" He was so careful that he began to count with himself and finished with himself.

"Now we have one too many," Todros murmured. "How come?"

They all wondered, "Who is the twenty-second man?"

Todros flared up. "Men, we have an impostor in our midst, an uninvited guest! A stranger smuggled himself into our exclusive club while we were talking! Who gave him the uniform?"

No one answered.

Todros began to shout. "The guilty party better step forward and confess if he knows what's good for him!"

Everyone denied the charge loudly and vehemently, but Todros shouted louder than all of them.

The rider heard the commotion and returned to the Helmites.

"What's the trouble now?"

"I counted just as you told me to, and now there's one too many. We have twenty-two men!"

"Let me see you count them."

Todros counted again, beginning with himself and finishing with himself.

The stranger looked at him for a moment and said with a smile, "Look here, the truth is that no matter who a man is, he must count himself as equal with others. If he doesn't count himself at all, no matter how lowly he is, a man is missing. On the other hand, no matter how important a man is, if he begins with himself and ends with himself, there is a superfluous man! One too many! Do you understand?"

"Not a word," answered Todros. "You know, I'm not a philosopher. I'm a practical man, the head of our most exclusive club. I have to protect our way of life. I have to see that our institutions are preserved and not destroyed by outsiders, by foreigners who don't understand or value the wisdom and the customs of Helm."

"I see," observed the horseman, "you're a practical man. So I have a practical plan. All of you lie down on the sand, face down. I'll give each one of you a lash with my whip. The first will cry, 'Ouch one,' the second, 'Ouch two,' and so on. Then you'll have no doubt about the counting. There just can't be any mistake."

The Helmites lay down on their bellies, next to one another, and the horseman began lashing, 'Ouch one!'—